THE GOOD-BYE YEAR

CAROLE BOLTON

LODESTAR BOOKS
E. P. Dutton   New York

Also by Carole Bolton

LITTLE GIRL LOST

THE SEARCH OF MARY KATHERINE MULLOY

Copyright © 1982 by Carole Bolton

LIBRARY OF CONGRESS CATALOGING IN PUBLICATION DATA
Bolton, Carole.
 The good-bye year.
 Summary: In the post-Depression year of 1939, thirteen-year-old Rosemary learns to accept many changes in her life including her father's employment away from home and a subsequent move to Baltimore when he returns.
 [1. Family problems—Fiction. 2. Moving, Household—Fiction] I. Title.
PZ7.B63596Go 1982   [Fic]   82-5043
ISBN 0-525-66787-3   AACR2

Published in the United States by E. P. Dutton, Inc.,
2 Park Avenue, New York, N.Y. 10016
Published simultaneously in Canada by Clarke,
Irwin & Company Limited, Toronto and Vancouver
Editor: Virginia Buckley   Designer: Trish Parcell
Printed in the U.S.A.   First Edition
10 9 8 7 6 5 4 3 2 1

*In loving memory
of my mother and father*

1

R *osemary Beedy, famous movie star, stood in the doorway of*
her studio bungalow the morning after receiving the Academy
Award. Reporters thronged around the beautiful star, but she was
modest and unaffected as she answered their eager questions.
Dressed in costume for a scene in her next picture, Queen Mary
of Scotland, *the actress was . . .*

Rosemary Beedy, walking home from her grandparents'
house with her pajamas and toothbrush in a paper bag on
this Friday evening, September 1, 1939, paused in her prog-
ress and looked furtively around. She had realized suddenly
that she was making faces as she daydreamed about Rosemary Beedy, famous star. But fortunately the street was
empty. If there had been people nearby they would have
seen an ordinary brown-haired schoolgirl. They could not
have known that Rosemary thought herself different from
everybody else.

Confident that she was unobserved, Rosemary continued
on her way and began imagining what she might be wear-

ing as Mary, Queen of Scots. Brocade, perhaps, made with gold thread and trimmed in jewels, with one of those dear little caps that framed the face so becomingly. Or maybe her clothing would be more severe, if the scene she was doing took place during Mary's imprisonment. Rosemary had been reading a book about Mary of Scots, and she felt she knew a great deal about her. She certainly knew that she would love to play her in a movie or play when she became famous.

She sighed, stopped, and leaned dreamily against a stone wall. Overhead the green of the sycamores had taken on a golden hue in the light of the sun, which was low now and approaching the tops of the mountains. But Rosemary, her mind far away from western Pennsylvania, did not notice, although she was vaguely aware somewhere within her fantasy that she had better get home and start dinner for herself and her mother.

Her mother had been in Pittsburgh for the past few days seeing about the affairs of Great-Aunt Millicent, who had died recently, but she was due home any minute. Since her grandmother had also gone, Rosemary had been keeping house for her grandfather, but she was glad now to be getting back to her own room, to her piles of movie magazines, scrapbooks, and photographs of the stars, and to her collection of books.

To her left the stone wall joined an iron gate, and she glanced in at the big empty house standing at the end of a long curving drive. The house, known as the Wakely house, was built partly of stone and partly of white stucco. The portico in front was supported by large white pillars that gave it the look of a Southern mansion, like Tara in *Gone With the Wind*. In fact, Rosemary always thought of Tara when she saw it. At thirteen, she had already read *Gone With the Wind* twice, since the memorable day a year ago when her mother had told her that she might enjoy it.

Rosemary grasped the iron gate and gazed at the house. On one side French doors opened out onto a terrace, where the owners, who had been gone for some years, might once have dined in good weather. The terrace itself had a good view of the swimming pool, empty now and with cracks in places, where weeds grew, and a crumbling tennis court, its frazzled net still lying on the ground.

Oh, it would be wonderful to live in such a place—or at least she supposed so, for Rosemary's feelings about the house were mixed. Part of her saw it as a place where long, hanging Spanish moss should grow, and ladies in hoop skirts walk sedately. Another part of her saw it as a mansion in a movie, where stars like Irene Dunne or Myrna Loy might lounge about in floor-length, figure-hugging, backless dresses, making witty remarks to Cary Grant or William Powell and drinking out of long-stemmed glasses.

But a third part of Rosemary, and perhaps the strongest part, had a completely different vision of the house. That part of her saw it as haunted. As long as she could remember, no one had ever lived in it. She had asked her mother about it once, and her mother said the people who owned the house had moved out at the beginning of the Depression, because they couldn't afford to keep it up, and no one had bought it, because no one else could afford to live there either.

Rosemary hadn't accepted that explanation, though. She was sure something had happened there, something frightening and terrible, that had left its mark on the place. In fact, her best friend, Ruth Marshall, said that a murder had been committed in the house. Mr. Wakely had been so upset when the stock market crashed and he lost all his money that one night he had shot his wife and two daughters to death and then killed himself.

But when Rosemary confronted her mother with this version of the story, her mother had merely laughed. "What a lurid imagination Ruth has!" she said.

Still, one night when Rosemary was sleeping over at Ruth's, Ruth had told her, "It's true, you know. He killed them just before daylight, just as the milkman was coming down the street. The milkman heard the shots, and he was so shocked that he dropped the whole rack of milk bottles, and the milk spilled all over the sidewalk." Ruth had paused for effect. "And you know what? The stain that milk made on the street *never went away*, no matter how often it rained."

Rosemary turned from the house and looked down at the street, but there was nothing on the sidewalk that resembled an old stain made by milk. She had often searched for it but had never found it. That was because, Ruth had told her blandly, the sidewalk had probably been repaved at some time in the past.

But there was more to the story Ruth had told her that night, her voice spooky and low in the darkness of the bedroom. "One of the girls—Aurora was her name—didn't die right away. She got up and stumbled toward the stairway—a long winding one—and she groped her way down it . . . sl-o-w-ly . . . looking for help, and her bloody hands left marks all along the wall until . . . she crumpled in a heap at the bottom of the stairs. Dead."

Ruth was silent. Rosemary felt a chill along her spine.

"And now," Ruth had continued, her voice even lower, "on dark stormy nights—or any night, especially on the anniversary of her death—Aurora can be heard moaning and wailing on the staircase, pleading for help that never comes. . . ."

The sun had almost disappeared behind the mountains, and for the first time Rosemary was aware of growing shadows, a hint of coming darkness. From the direction of the house a slight breeze arose and fanned her face, bringing with it—or so she thought—a smell of dampness and decay. Overhead in a large oak tree, which grew on the other side of the wall but spread its branches over the sidewalk, a flock of birds had congregated, chirping loudly and excitedly as if they were holding a meeting, with everyone talking at once. Suddenly they all took to the air in a great windy thunder of wings.

Rosemary's heart gave a leap. She was sure she saw something flutter at the side of the house, like diaphanous clothing blowing or a hand beckoning. The roots of her hair prickled and she went cold all over. The next moment she was running away from the house, across the street, and then, at the corner, down the hill.

Partway down she stopped for breath, her sides heaving in and out, her lungs burning, and as she did, she heard a voice say, "Hey, Rosemary!"

Ruth was sitting on the top step of the porch of her house. Rosemary, still panting, walked over to her and sat down on a bottom step. "Hi," she said.

"Was someone chasing you?" asked Ruth, who was a sturdy, plumpish girl with tightly permanented blonde hair.

"I just felt like running," Rosemary said. She glanced up at the magazine Ruth was holding in her lap, with its garish cover carefully folded inward. "Is that the new *Weird Tales* you've got? Is it good?"

"I don't know. I've just started it. But I'll lend it to you when I get through." Ruth hid the magazine, cover side down, under the edge of her skirt in case they were interrupted by her mother, who, Rosemary knew, highly disapproved of it. "Been to your grandparents'?" Ruth asked. "I'm glad you're finally back."

"I am, too," said Rosemary. "There isn't much time left to do things, with school starting the day after Labor Day. What about the movie tomorrow? Are you going away for the weekend?"

"No," said Ruth. "I'll be here." Then she exclaimed suddenly, "Oh, say! Guess what happened while you were at your grandparents'! Your house has been rented."

Rosemary's insides gave a twist; she frowned. "Oh? How do you know?"

"I saw them moving in today."

"Is that so?" Rosemary could not share Ruth's excitement. She still felt proprietary about her previous home. Three months ago her father had gone away to travel as a clarinetist with a dance band. Some people said he had

6

abandoned his family, although she and her mother knew differently. Just the same, soon after he went away they had had to move out of their house, because he couldn't send them enough money to live on and they couldn't afford the rent. They were now living across the street from that house in three rooms that they rented from Mrs. Hauser.

As long as her old house was empty, Rosemary had not felt so bad about it, but now the thought of someone else playing in the big backyard, someone else sleeping in *her* room . . . well, it hurt.

"Do they have any kids our age?" she managed to say.

"*Near* our age," said Ruth. "It's the Mitchells. Remember them? Remember Mitch—the boy they called Mitch?"

"They moved away a long time ago," Rosemary said evasively, for she did not want to admit that she remembered Mitch perfectly, although she hadn't thought of him for years—and that even after all that time she remembered him with unmixed feelings of sheer dislike. All sorts of unpleasant feelings were sweeping over her. Mitch in *her* house!

Abruptly she got up from the step. "Ruth, I've got to go. My mother's probably back."

"OK, I'll be seeing you tomorrow anyway," said Ruth. "Gum-bye."

Rosemary ran the rest of the way down the hill. When she reached the bottom she stopped on Mrs. Hauser's porch and stared across the street. The front door of the house where she had once lived was standing open behind its screen, and upstairs windows were open too. Although that seemed more natural than the closed-up look that had prevailed since she and her mother had left, a lump rose in her throat.

And Mitch lived there now. *Mitch!*

Even as Rosemary watched, the screen door opened and a boy came out. She could not see him very well in the shadows under the trees—and she didn't want to be caught staring—but he seemed broad-shouldered and tall. Rosemary hadn't remembered that Mitch had a brother. This must be a brother, because Mitch had been small for his age.

The boy hadn't noticed her standing on the porch as he sauntered, slouched a bit, hands in his pockets, toward Wallace Boulevard, and she was glad he hadn't. He might mention it to Mitch.

Slowly she turned and went into the Hauser house. A sharp bark greeted her as she turned the knob, but when she entered, a wet tongue immediately licked her hand in recognition.

She bent and patted the Hausers' fox terrier. "Hello, Bingo," she said.

Mrs. Hauser came from the direction of the kitchen. She was a large woman, extremely well padded, with a no-nonsense air about her. Rosemary always felt a little afraid of Mrs. Hauser. She had a huge puff of coal-black hair on her head, which Rosemary suspected was a wig. However, Mrs. Hauser had told Rosemary's mother that it was a "transformation," whatever that was. Rosemary supposed it did transform her.

Rosemary glanced down at the hall table where the mail was kept. "Hello, Mrs. Hauser," she said, and she picked up a letter addressed to her mother in her father's handwriting.

"There's a letter from your father," Mrs. Hauser said. "I hope he sent your mother some money, poor little thing."

"Er . . . yes," said Rosemary, embarrassed.

"She isn't back yet," Mrs. Hauser informed her.

"Oh? I thought she would be . . . Well, I'll get supper started anyway."

Mrs. Hauser smiled in the grim way she had. "That's a good girl," she said, and she went back to her kitchen. Rosemary started up the stairs with a sense of having escaped from some nameless dread. She didn't know why, but she always felt vaguely guilty around Mrs. Hauser.

Up in her mother's bedroom, which they also used as a living room, Rosemary turned on the radio and a light, then went into the room on the other side of the stairs that was their kitchen. It had a refrigerator and a stove, but water for dishes had to be carried from the bathroom down the hall, which ran at a right angle from the stairwell. Rosemary's tiny bedroom was along the hall too, just past the door of Mrs. Hauser's other roomer, a thin dark woman named Malvina, who worked for Fine's Department Store.

Rosemary opened the refrigerator door, but found little there besides a few eggs. Well, that's what they would have. A lot of people in these hard times would be happy with a dinner consisting of scrambled eggs and toast.

Rosemary got out the eggs and started setting the table, but her mind was only half on what she was doing. Mostly she was thinking about Mitch Mitchell. She had thought he was out of her life forever after his family moved to West

Virginia. Now they were back, right across the street, and in her own house, too, to make matters worse. She had no hope that four years had improved Mitch in the slightest. If anything, he was probably more hateful than ever.

2

Rosemary had *never* liked Mitch, but the whole trouble with him had begun when she was about nine and Mitch about twelve. One evening in early August a game of cowboys had got started on the street just above Rosemary's house. Rosemary was the only girl in the neighborhood who was around that night, and she was also younger than the boys, who did not conceal their distaste at having her tag along. Still, tag along she did, and finally Roger Lipman, a boy from the next street, said she could be on his side. Mitch Mitchell and his roughneck buddies made up the other side.

At first they had raced around the immediate neighborhood, through backyards and over fences, and then the game had ranged farther afield.

Roger called a conference of his team. "They're hiding out in the old cemetery up on Washington Hill," he told them. "I know they are. I think we ought to send a scout to make sure, and then when he comes back and reports, we can go and blast them."

Rosemary began jumping up and down. "Let *me* go, Roger. Let *me* go!" she cried out breathlessly. Excitement had flushed her face, and her forehead was damp with perspiration. She almost believed that the game was for real. "Let me be a scout, Roger. I'll do a good job."

Roger looked down at her and scowled, but at last he said, "All right, but just make sure you don't get caught. This is a rough game for girls."

"I'll be careful, Roger."

Bursting with importance at her charge, Rosemary had thrust her cap pistol into its holster and started up the hill. She kept as close to the houses as she could and ducked one by one from the cover of a porch here, a tree there, until at the top of the hill she saw the ancient cemetery following the curve of the road as it sloped down in the opposite direction from the Wakely house and Mountain Street toward the railroad tracks. Beneath tall old trees the white, weather-beaten, sunken gravestones gleamed in the gathering darkness. Rosemary sucked in her breath. The moment was so serious that she was shaking all over with tension.

She could see no movement anywhere and had begun to think Mitch and his pals weren't there, when suddenly strong hands gripped her arms from both sides, pinioning them painfully behind her. Rosemary shrieked.

"Caught you!" said a boy's triumphant voice. Then he laughed harshly. "We saw you coming a mile away. Hey, Mitch," he called. "We caught a spy."

Struggling with her captors, Rosemary was dragged across the road and through the underbrush into the neglected cemetery. There, hidden by tree trunks and sitting on the ground, their backs against the tombstones, was the whole enemy group. When they saw Rosemary, they got to their feet and pointed their toy revolvers and wooden rifles in her direction. Mitch, the leader, came forward a little, his hair flaming even in the shadows.

"Just that dumb little girl," he said. "What do we want with her?"

"She was spying, Mitch. They sent her."

He put his face close to Rosemary's. "Did they, kid?"

"I'm not talking," she said belligerently.

Mitch stood up straight. He was no taller than anyone else, but he gave an impression of sturdiness. "Take her hardware," he ordered. One of his friends pulled Rosemary's cap pistol out of its holster and tossed it to Mitch, who stuck it in his belt.

"Hey," said Rosemary. "That's mine."

"Can't let you have a gun. You might hurt yourself," said Mitch.

Shocked tears stung Rosemary's eyes; she fought them back with difficulty. He wasn't playing fair. People didn't take other people's guns in games, no matter what real cowboys did.

While two boys continued to hold her, Mitch went into a huddle with the rest. They talked for a minute, the younger boys snickering over what was said. Then Mitch came back. "Tie her up," he said.

Before Rosemary could even protest, they had shoved her to the ground, her back against one of the gravestones. Then they twisted her arms behind the stone and tied them. Rosemary laughed nervously. It was exciting in a way. The game was just like a Buck Jones movie. The hero had been caught by the outlaws. She tried to smile as she pulled at the rope, which was much too secure for her liking.

Mitch had been squatting down, inspecting the knots. Now he stood up and said with satisfaction, "That'll hold." Eyes shining, he looked down at his captive. "We'll teach you to think you can outsmart us," he told her. His lip curled in a tough grimace that he had obviously practiced. "This is no game for girls," he said.

Then, from somewhere far off, a voice began calling, "Bil-ly! Bil-lee!"

"Hey," said a boy. "I have to go."

"Me too," said someone else. "Wait for me, Bill. So long, you guys." And without further ado, they both ran off.

"Heck. What's the use of playing if everybody's leaving," said Mitch. He shrugged. "Come on," he said, and he and the other boys slowly started off after the two who had already left. Nobody gave Rosemary a backward glance.

"Wait! What about me?" she shouted. She was half crying now, and she hoped that Mitch wouldn't notice that.

"What *about* you?" He came back and stared down at her again. His face looked mean as he gave a little kick at her outstretched leg. "You'll get loose if you try hard enough. We didn't tie you *that* tight. And when you do," he added, "you can tell those other dumb kids that we've all gone home because we won. See?" He took Rosemary's cap pistol out of his belt and twirled it more or less expertly around a dirty index finger.

"You give that back!" she demanded.

"Come and get it then," Mitch taunted her. He aimed at a tree and shot off a few caps.

Hearing shots, his friends came back. "Come on, Mitch. Stop fooling around."

"Sure," said Mitch. He stuck the gun back in his belt. "So long, crybaby," he said. "Next time play with the girls." Laughing, he turned around and ran after his friends, and immediately the darkness under the trees swallowed him up.

For a long time Rosemary could hear shouts and laughter, but gradually they died away, then stopped altogether. Alone now, she pulled and twisted at the rope, which cut painfully into her wrists. She tried to raise herself and bring her arms up over the top of the stone behind her, but it was too high and her position was too awkward for her to do that. Sobbing gently, she sat there, out of breath, and as she grew still, she realized that everything around her was quiet now too, except for a car moving down Washington Street in the distance. Darkest night had suddenly descended upon her. The trees spread their branches over her head, and for a moment the wind rushed through their leaves with a sound like many voices talking—like the voices of the dead, she thought in terror, staring at the graves all around her. What if, all at once, they opened up and the dead people came out?

Why, she was even sitting on a grave! Whose grave? She had no way of knowing, because she was leaning against the stone. But what if the ground gave way underneath her and she was dragged down into the coffin?

Rosemary was close to fainting in her panic. Tears mingled with the dirt and sweat on her face. "Help!" she cried. "Help! Help!" The words trailed off into a wail of elemental fear.

The struggle to free herself was exhausting her. Where the rope had cut into her wrists she felt something warm and wet and sticky. It might be blood, but she just didn't care. She *had* to get free, and she sobbed and moaned as she struggled with the rope.

It seemed to take forever, but her frantic fight eventually freed her. When she felt the rope finally loosen, she pulled it off, stood up and, tottering at first, broke into a run. And she did not stop running until she was well away from the cemetery and under a street lamp in her own neighborhood. There she came to a halt and rested her hot sobbing lungs, her arms wound around the metal post, her whole body shaking, while the hatred in her heart for Mitch Mitchell grew and grew.

3

The radio had been blaring in the living room. Lowell Thomas had begun to comment on the news. He was excited about something involving Poland, but Rosemary wasn't listening very hard. She was too busy remembering Mitch Mitchell. Besides, her mother should be home from Pittsburgh by this time. Rosemary went to the front room and pulled the curtain aside, but there was no sign of her. She was, however, rewarded with the sight of the back of Mitch's brother as he went up the steps and reentered the house, a paper bag in his hand.

Rosemary dropped the curtain and moved away from the window. Her stomach had clamped into a tight fist of fore-boding. With Mitch right across the street, she would have to see him every day—or nearly every day. How could she avoid it? And because of that, she would be reminded every day of the worst humiliation of her life.

It *had* been humiliating, too. Everybody else involved might have forgotten it by now, perhaps even Mitch himself, but Rosemary remembered. The details were all coming back now, vividly.

The night after Mitch and his pals left her tied up in the cemetery, Rosemary had draped her belt with its empty holster over the bottom of her bed. She had wanted to have it where she would see it in the morning and remember how her property had been stolen from her. How she was going to get her cap pistol back she did not know, but get it back she would.

The next morning, as soon as breakfast was over, she trotted up the hill in the sunshine to an empty lot across from Mitch's house, where she knew he often hung out. Just as she had expected, Mitch was there, playing marbles with some other boys. Rosemary stood watching them, but they all acted as if she were invisible. Mitch had once condescended to let Rosemary play marbles with him when there was nobody else to play with, and she had not held it against him when he had won all she had, even though she had just bought the marbles that very day. In fact, the little net bag they had come in was still stiff and new.

Rosemary did not have any marbles today, so Mitch had no interest in her. "See anybody?" he asked his friends. They laughed.

Mitch had won the marbles fair and square, but Rosemary did not intend to let him get away with *stealing* something from her. "Mitch Mitchell," she said, "I want my cap pistol back."

"Did you hear somebody?" said Mitch.

"No, I didn't hear anybody," said one of his friends. They went on with their game.

"Give me my cap pistol, Mitch," Rosemary said, her voice rising in inflection.

When Mitch did not answer, anger flared up in her. She could feel her face getting hot. She stamped a foot down in front of them and, scattering marbles, used it angrily, contemptuously, to rub out the circle they had drawn on the ground with a stick.

"Give it to me, Mitch!"

"Cut that out!" Mitch shouted. He grabbed her ankle and pulled on it so roughly that Rosemary sat down, hard. "I don't have *your* cap pistol," he said, "because it's mine now. And just you remember that, kid. If you're going to be a pest and play with boys, you've got to abide by the rules."

"What rules? Who made them?" Rosemary started to hit him, the thumps of her fists on his chest giving her immense satisfaction.

Mitch caught her wrists.

Rosemary yanked away. "Come on and fight, you coward!" she yelled.

Mitch stood up, knocking her sideways. His eyes were hard, like two grayish-green marbles. "I don't fight with little girls. Go and play jacks with the other babies." He started to walk away, beckoning his friends to follow. "Let's get out of here," he said. "This neighborhood stinks."

"You're afraid," Rosemary taunted him. "You're afraid

a girl might beat you up. Well, I challenge you, Mr. Mitch Mitchell."

Mitch kept on walking. But his friends were talking to him; they were laughing. She heard Mitch say, "I am *not!*" Then he turned around and looked at her. Rosemary put her hands on her hips and stuck out her tongue.

"Scaredy-cat," she sang. "Scared of a girl. Come on, I'll fight you for my gun. *I'm* not afraid."

"What makes you think I am?" Mitch asked. He glanced from one to the other of his friends. Then he looked down the street, where the Baptist minister was washing his car. "Well, not here," he added. "I'll meet you in back of my house after lunch. And if you can lick me, kid, I'll give you your old cap pistol back."

Rosemary thought she had never seen anybody look as mean as Mitch did when he turned and walked away with his buddies. She began to feel a little nervous. But she wasn't afraid, she told herself. She could beat up that awful boy anywhere, given a fair chance.

That afternoon Rosemary sallied forth to the fray eagerly. She went by way of the alley, so no one would see her and wonder what she was up to. The day was a hot one, with scorching sunlight reflecting up from the alley. Hollyhocks and sunflowers drowsed over the fences in some of the backyards. Hydrangea bushes in full bloom drooped with their load of white snowballs. Rosemary walked past them, her head high. Past the garbage cans and the garages she went. At Mitch's house the garage door was open, and she could see Mitch in there with his friends. He had his bike turned over and was doing something with the chain.

"I'm here, and I want my gun," she said. "If I have to fight you for it, I will."

Mitch looked up, and his face reddened.

One of the other boys laughed. "Go on, Mitch," he said. "Teach the little brat a lesson."

Rosemary thrust out her lower lip as Mitch stood there indecisively. Not until she had drawn blood would she feel satisfied. She knew he didn't want to fight her because she was a girl and much younger than he was. Well, she wasn't going to let him use that as an excuse.

Before Mitch could say or do anything, she lowered her head and charged. As she plowed into his stomach, Mitch gave out a grunt and sat down on the floor of the garage. The power of her lunge made Rosemary keep on going. She fell against one of the other boys, and he gave her a push. "Hey, Mitch, here she is!"

Spinning around, Rosemary wobbled back toward Mitch. He was up now and waiting for her, his fists clenched. But as she came toward him, his hand opened. Instead of punching her as she expected, he slapped her sharply across the face. Stunned, her cheek stinging, she stopped and looked at him.

"Had enough?" yelled Mitch. "Then go home. I don't want to hurt you."

He was shouting, angry with himself as much as with Rosemary, but his words hardly penetrated. Rosemary was conscious of nothing but her own fury. She *did* want to hurt him; she *would* hurt him.

She threw herself upon Mitch, her arms flailing. She tried to remember to keep her hands clenched, but they kept opening and she found that most of the time she was using the age-old female tactic of scratching. Her nails went down his face, leaving a red mark behind. Mitch grabbed her hands and started twisting her arm. In a blur of pain, she saw his face and suddenly realized that he knew his honor was at stake. If he had to fight a girl, he couldn't let her beat him.

But maybe she would, she thought in triumph as she broke his hold on her.

She had hardly thought that when Mitch launched a counterattack. He grabbed her around the waist and pulled her tightly against him as if he were hugging her. Instead, he began to spank her as hard as he could. Rosemary struggled, but his grip was like iron and the spanking went on and on. No one had ever spanked her as long or as hard as this.

The circle of boys around them laughed and shouted encouragement to Mitch who, again, had not played fair. He was punishing her, not fighting her as he would an equal. Degraded, furious, Rosemary made a desperate effort and finally broke away from him, but Mitch was after her in a moment. He caught her by the shoulders and proceeded to shake her. Her head bobbled back and forth, and she felt her teeth rattle. She snatched at his arm for support, afraid she was going to fall down. If he didn't stop, she was going to be sick.

And all at once he did stop, and looked down at her. "Go home," he said. "And don't let me catch you around here again." He let her go, and the boys made way for him as he walked away from her over toward his bike. He stood looking down at it, his back to her, and he did not turn around again.

Rosemary swayed dizzily. She was still afraid she might throw up. She could feel the boys staring at her, but no one said a word. Drunkenly she moved toward the door, and the boys opened their ranks to let her pass. Behind her she heard someone giggle, a belittling sound, full of contempt. After that they were silent again. They felt she had stepped beyond the bounds and tried to enter their world, and she had not been strong enough. Now she was filled with self-loathing—not because she had fought, but because she had lost!

Humiliated, she slowly left the scene, and their silence followed her the whole way. Only when she reached home and had hidden herself under the porch did she dare indulge in the great luxury of bawling, because now she would never be able to face those boys again—especially Mitch Mitchell. He was the one who had done it, who had made her feel so low.

And Rosemary never did play with the boys again. What was more important, she carefully avoided Mitch Mitchell from that day on. It wasn't that she was afraid of him. She knew he wouldn't hurt her, that he had never wanted to hurt her. But she didn't want to meet his eyes and see in them the remembrance of her moment of degradation.

Therefore, when Mitch's family moved to West Virginia, Rosemary had felt as though a great burden had been lifted from her life.

4

Rosemary came back to the present with a jolt. Lowell Thomas was going off the air with his familiar "So long, until tomorrow," and she hadn't heard a word he said. Her mother wasn't home yet, either, and it was seven o'clock. Where *was* she? Rosemary was starving.

"Amos and Andy" came on, but Rosemary wasn't all that interested. She changed stations and found some music, a swing band playing "Deep Purple." Softly humming along with it, she returned to the kitchen and again looked inside the refrigerator. Mere scrambled eggs no longer appealed to her; she craved something with a little more character.

I know, she thought, fried-egg-and-onion sandwiches. She removed the jar of mustard from the refrigerator and found a big onion.

She sliced the onion, and her eyes began to water, so she ran back to the living room to her mother's mirror to see how she looked with tears in her eyes. A stricken expression came over her face as she brandished the knife and the onion dramatically. "Oh, Charles!" she mouthed. "Don't leave me!"

Then she heard the door downstairs close gently. Some-one was coming up the steps.

"Mother?" Rosemary ran to the top of the stairs, the knife and onion still in her hands.

"Sh, I don't want Mrs. Hauser to hear me."

"Why not?" Rosemary whispered back.

Anne Beedy was a slender, delicate-looking woman of thirty-three, with large brown eyes. She came up the stairs toward Rosemary, then pecked her on the cheek before going into the living room. In one hand she carried her overnight bag; in the other was a squat-looking black case with a kind of mesh covering at one end. She dropped the bag on the floor and placed the case in a chair.

Rosemary leaned over the case. From its depths two shiny, slanted, mint-green eyes stared out at her. "What's that?" she asked.

"Now what does it look like?" said her mother. "It's a cat."

"Great-Aunt Millicent's cat?"

"Who else's?" Her mother plopped down on the sofa and sighed. She looked tired.

"You mean Aunt Millicent left us her cat?" said Rose-mary. "Isn't that wonderful!" She knelt down and started to release the catch on the door of the case.

"Wonderful?" repeated her mother in a sarcastic voice. "Rosemary, close the door to the hall before you let it out."

Rosemary jumped up to obey. Then, eagerly, she opened

the case. "Come on out, kitty," she cajoled. As the cat cautiously emerged from its confinement, Rosemary picked it up and tried to stroke it. The animal protested loudly and dug razorlike claws into her shoulder. "Ow-w!" said Rosemary. "Cut that out, cat! Come on now, let me have a look at you. I'm not going to hurt you. What's it called, Mother?"

"Thompson," she said. "I don't know where Aunt Milly dug up such an unsuitable name."

"Thompson . . . Why, I think that's the same cat she had that time you and Gramma took me to visit her. I remember that name."

"Yes, he's almost ten years old now." Her mother rose wearily and put her hat and pocketbook away. She sat down at her dressing table in the bedroom part of the big room and ran a comb through her cloud of fine, naturally curly brown hair, hair that her daughter envied, because she had inherited the color and the fineness but not the natural curl.

Rosemary carefully unhooked Thompson's claws from her blouse and held him up for a better look. He was a larger-than-average black-and-white alley cat. He had a black mask around his green eyes and what resembled a black mustache. All four feet were white.

"She should have named him Boots," said Rosemary.

Across the room the comb caught in her mother's hair, and she dropped it on the floor with a clatter. The cat twisted in fright from Rosemary's grasp and left a long scratch on her arm, from which blood began to ooze in a dotted line of tiny drops.

"Hey!" she protested. She glared as Thompson scurried under the coffee table and then under the couch. "A better name for him would have been Hitler, with that mustache and bad disposition."

"That's more appropriate than you know," her mother said gloomily.

"Oh? What do you mean?"

"He's going to be dictating our lives, I'm afraid . . . for a while, anyway."

"No kidding. You mean Aunt Millicent left him all her money?"

"That's right. Almost right, I mean."

"Aw, go on," said Rosemary. "I didn't know Aunt Millicent even had any money."

"Well, there's the house," said her mother, coming back over to her, "which is worth about three or four thousand. And there's over two thousand in the bank. She had a small insurance policy that will cover the funeral expenses." Her mother paused. "Most of it she left to your grandmother, of course, but a thousand of it comes to me . . . if I . . . if we . . . Well, under certain conditions."

Anne Beedy's big brown eyes were serious, almost awed, as she stared at Rosemary. Rosemary's father had been out of work for several months before he joined the dance band and started touring the country. The money he sent back to them had not been enough for them to live on, hence their move to these rooms, but they were still having a hard time making ends meet. Although Anne Beedy planned to start work as a clerk in an office downtown the day after Labor Day, it would be a while before they felt the benefits of that new income. For all these reasons, a thousand dollars seemed like a fortune.

Rosemary glanced in sudden violent distaste at the cat, which had slunk across the floor and was now crying at the door.

"She *couldn't* have left all that money to—to what's-his-name."

"Thompson," said her mother.

"I know."

"Well, she didn't, exactly. She left it to me, but there are strings attached. You see, Aunt Milly was very fond of her cat; he was the only thing she had to love, you know. And, after all, aside from being lonely, she was pretty eccentric. She stressed in her will that she didn't want him put to death. And she couldn't leave him to Mother, because Mother hates cats, as you well know. That left me, and actually, if it hadn't been for the cat, I don't think she'd have mentioned me in her will at all."

"So?"

"I'm afraid she remembered, Rosemary, that you had teased her cat that time we took you to visit her."

"I did?" said Rosemary. "Why, I was only a little kid then, for Pete's sake. I don't remem— Oh, wait a minute. I *knew* there was a reason why that name Thompson stayed in my mind all that time. I *liked* him—that was it—and I wanted to cuddle him. I picked him up and he scratched me, and Aunt Milly yelled at me. But I was the one who should have been mad, not her!"

"She didn't see it that way, I guess, and that's what counts." Her mother sighed. "Anyway, no one is really to blame. She would probably have done it just the same."

"Done what? That's what I want to know," said Rosemary.

"She left a thousand dollars to me," said her mother, as if reciting a piece she had learned. "For one year I must take good care of her cat and let nothing happen to him. If, at the end of that year, he is alive and well—or has died *only* of natural causes—I will have proved myself a good owner for him, and the thousand dollars will be mine. At no time, however, unless he is suffering, is Thompson to be put to sleep."

A deep silence settled between them. They both watched as Thompson, who had given up on the door, clawed at the screen in one of the windows and yowled. Rosemary realized vaguely that his claw was stuck, but she made no move to help him. She felt paralyzed.

"What are natural causes?" she asked softly. "And what if he should die of *un*natural ones? What if he is alive, but is *un*well?"

"If he's unwell naturally, that's all right, but if he's unnaturally dead, the money goes to the Home for Homeless Felines."

Rosemary stared at her. "What in the world is that?"

Her mother laughed, as the humor of their situation suddenly struck her. "Aunt Milly's best friend takes in strays. She has about sixteen cats at present, and I think the name is something she and Aunt Milly cooked up between them for the purposes of the will."

Rosemary watched without sympathy as Thompson struggled with the screen. "You'd think," she said, "that

Aunt Milly would have left Thompson and the money to her."

"No," explained her mother with a grin, "she wanted Thompson to have individual attention."

"Good grief," Rosemary said. In a daze she stepped over to Thompson, extricated his claw from the screen, and dumped him on the floor. "Can't you—what do they call it? —contest the will?"

"Well," said her mother, brushing a stray hair off her forehead, "Aunt Milly wrote the will herself, by hand, but she had it witnessed, and it's all perfectly legal, the lawyer says. It's going to be entered for probate, but he'll do all he can to see if we can waive the conditions. But actively contesting it would take time and money, and we haven't any of the latter, you know that, Rosemary."

Rosemary made a face. "I guess we'll just have to take care of the silly animal, that's all," she said.

"All right, but just remember, Rosemary, that we must never let Thompson out of the house. He might get hit by a car or poisoned or something." Her mother removed the onion from the coffee table where Rosemary had placed it. "My, that smells good," she said. "Let's have something to eat. We still have to talk to Mrs. Hauser tonight and get her permission for him to stay. If she won't allow it— Oh, I simply don't want to think about that until after supper. I haven't eaten since breakfast."

Rosemary followed her to the kitchen, leaving Thompson shut in the living room. "No one in Lynnfield keeps a cat in the house all the time," she said.

"Well, Aunt Milly kept Thompson in the house, and

we'll have to do the same thing. He's used to a box of sand."

Thompson meowed piteously at the door.

Rosemary put the skillet on the stove. "What fun it's going to be—being careful all the time and telling your friends to be careful—just so Thompson doesn't escape."

Thompson gave another meow at the door.

"Maybe I ought to feed him," suggested Rosemary.

"Wait till he calms down," said her mother.

"That's right. We don't want him to choke, do we?" Rosemary said.

"A ten-year-old cat could die of almost anything," said her mother thoughtfully.

They made the sandwiches and took them, along with glasses of milk, into the living room to eat. Thompson circled the room, jumped on the bed, then returned to the door once more and sniffed at it, crying.

"Poor little thing," said her mother. "He misses Aunt Milly."

Rosemary said nothing. She looked at Thompson, who did not look like a poor little thing at all. He had sat down and was now washing vigorously. When he looked up, his eyes were angry, frustrated, spitting fire.

Rosemary loved all animals and even as a small child had never treated them with anything but gentleness, despite what Aunt Millicent might have thought. She resented Thompson for hurting her reputation and for putting them in this position in the first place. If it hadn't been for his bad temper years ago, they would have had the thousand dollars without any complications. Or would they? Maybe not. At any rate, it existed for them now, and because of it they would have to watch this cat every minute, never really having any peace of mind. Cats were such independent, devious creatures, too! And money really was the root of all evil.

Of one thing she was certain, though: She did not have to *like* Thompson. And she didn't like him. In fact, she hated him. Now that he had finished his ablutions he had turned his back on them and sat staring up toward the windows as if he saw something outside that was hidden to human eyes. As she looked at that broad black back, she saw his ears twitch. He was aware of her notice, and the contempt in his attitude was unmistakable; there was no doubt that he knew he was the king of the cats.

"Well . . ." said Mrs. Hauser, after Rosemary and her mother had explained their problem to her after supper, "this is certainly an unusual situation."

"Yes, I know it is, but Rosemary and I will make very sure that Thompson isn't a bit of trouble."

"I suppose," said their landlady, "there's no way to get around it. Of course," she added sternly, "we would have to keep the door to the stairs closed. In fact, everyone would have to make sure to, so he and Bingo wouldn't get into a fight. I wouldn't want the dog to get scratched. Earle dotes on him, you know."

"Yes, I know."

At the sound of his name, Mr. Hauser walked out of the living room and joined them in the hallway. He was a dapper little man in a vest, shorter and smaller than his wife, with a receding hairline and a tiny, neat brown mustache. He and Bingo looked very much alike.

"Hello, ladies," he said. "Did you hear the news? Hitler has invaded Poland."

"Oh, dear!" said Rosemary's mother.

"Sure to mean war over there," he went on. "I just hope we keep out of it this time, but you never know what that Roosevelt will do next."

"He doesn't want war either, Earle," said his wife. Then, getting back to the matter at hand, she explained to him about Thompson. "What do you think? Is it all right with you?"

"Oh, sure," he said. He smiled. "Just keep him away from old Bingo. Bingo hates cats, you know."

"Well, then, that's settled," said Mrs. Hauser. "But, Anne, you'd better talk to Malvina. After all, her room is upstairs too. And she has a right to say whether she will share her home with a cat. Is he clean?"

"Oh, yes!" Anne Beedy said hastily. "Very. Aunt Millicent was strict about that."

"All right, then," Mrs. Hauser said in her heavy way, "providing Malvina agrees, we'll give it a try. I can see how much it must mean to you. After all, you can have the beast put to sleep once the year is up—that's one consolation."

"Yes," said Anne. "Thank you." She and Rosemary retreated to the stairway and carefully closed the door at the bottom behind them.

Once they were back in their own rooms, Rosemary exploded. "Put him to sleep! How can she think that way?"

She looked over at the bed where Thompson lay curled on top of her mother's pillow. He cast an indifferent, sleepy eye at her, then snuggled his nose more closely into the warmth of his tail. "It isn't fair!"

"No, it doesn't seem so, does it?" said her mother. "But we at least ought to be thankful that Mrs. Hauser is giving him a chance."

"The old dragon!"

"Rosemary, that's no way to talk. She tries to be kind."

"Oh, I know. It's just that I hate living here. I hate having to worry about what the Hausers think all the time."

"So do I." Her mother sighed with feeling. "But we were lucky to have this place available—and so cheaply."

"Grampa and Gramma would let us live with them. They asked us to. It would be so much nicer than these awful rooms."

"No!" Her mother's voice was sharp. "We have privacy here, Rosemary, in spite of Mrs. Hauser. I love my parents, but I'll never live with them again. Now say no more about it."

So that was the end of that, Rosemary supposed. They would just have to see that Thompson didn't annoy Malvina, and the Hausers, and Bingo—especially Bingo.

However, when Malvina came home later that night, she said she wouldn't mind at all. "I like cats," she said, stroking Thompson, who, strangely enough, didn't seem to mind. He yawned and stretched and looked up at her almost pleasantly. Malvina smiled. She was a tall young woman with a shape like an ironing board, and she was thin to the point of emaciation, with deep shadows under her black eyes. Yet when she smiled, she looked almost pretty. You could see that if she were a little more filled out, she would be fairly nice looking. Rosemary wondered if she got enough to eat.

"Thompson can visit me anytime he likes," Malvina told Rosemary. "Don't you worry about him. We'll see that he doesn't bother the Hausers."

She smiled again and went to her room. Rosemary's mother stared after her thoughtfully, but didn't say anything. Then she gave a little laugh and said to Rosemary, "We'd better get a pan ready for this cat. We'll use the bottom of the old roaster. You'll have to go down to the yard, Rosemary, and dig up some dirt."

"Oh, for heaven's sake!"

"It's only for a year, as Mrs. Hauser says. Or would you like to have the beast put to sleep now?"

"Oh, all right!" Rosemary said. "I get the point. Only don't rub it in." She paused at the threshold. "By the way, where are we going to put it? The pan, I mean."

"Why, in your room, of course."

"Mother!"

"Well, it doesn't belong in the kitchen—and we certainly can't have it in the living room. And Malvina uses the bathroom, so we can't put it there."

"If you ask me, Thompson is going to be a real pain in the neck," said Rosemary, turning away.

Before getting the pan from the kitchen, however, she went back to her own room to see where she would put it. There was only one place for it, the room was so small, she thought with a sigh: the few inches between the dresser and the window. Having it there, she thought, meant that any breath of air that wafted through the window from the three feet or so of shadowy space that separated the Hauser house from the one next door would have to blow over Thompson's pan first. How tawdry life was!

Rosemary groaned softly and stared at herself in the mirror. The brown eyes, so like her mother's, looked big and lost in the light of the dressing-table lamp, and her brown hair, straggly from need of a permanent, was also in want of brushing. She frowned at herself and picked up the brush. As she did so, her eye fell on her photograph of William Holden. She had only recently sent for it, so it still had an aura of newness, and the words "To Rosemary, with all good wishes, William Holden," still had the power to thrill her.

Ruth said that movie stars never autographed their own pictures, that secretaries or somebody did it, but Rosemary preferred to think that this was William Holden's own signature. She rubbed her finger over it gently and kissed the finger. Then, after giving her hair a few brisk brushes, she dropped the brush and went to the kitchen to look for the old baking pan.

5

Rosemary was sitting at the kitchen table eating cold kidney beans out of the can when Ruth stopped by for her the following morning at eleven thirty.

"What are you eating that stuff for?" Ruth asked.

"I like it," said Rosemary, who truly did. Kidney beans were a secret passion.

"Well, everybody to his own taste," said Ruth, "as the old woman said when she kissed the cow. Hey! Where'd that come from?"

Thompson was sitting in the living-room doorway, looking over at Ruth with his ears back and an expression of suspicion and dislike on his triangular face.

"Oh . . ." Rosemary waved her hand negligently. "He was my aunt's who died."

"Hm," said Ruth. "It's funny you can have *him*, when you had to give up Jiggs."

"I know," said Rosemary, but she didn't want to talk about Jiggs. She had been trying not to think about him ever since Thompson arrived, because the memory of him still hurt too much. Jiggs, a toy Boston bulldog, had been her very own, but when they moved over here, Mrs. Hauser had said she didn't want any more dogs in the house, and so Rosemary had had to give her pet away. She supposed she and her mother ought to thank their stars Thompson had been permitted to stay. He wouldn't have been, of course, if not for the special circumstances. But she would rather have had Jiggs.

"I'll tell you about the cat later," she said. She hurriedly finished her lunch, so she and Ruth would get to the theater on time. The movie today, *Wuthering Heights,* promised to be a good one.

She and Ruth reached the theater well before its Saturday opening time of noon. They were, in fact, the first in line. They bought their tickets—Rosemary's grandfather always saw to it that she had movie money—and entered the outer lobby, where posters for next week's attractions were set in gilt frames between the mirrors that covered both walls. Virgil, the ticket taker, guarded the entrance to the inner lobby with the tall receptacle into which he dropped his half of each ticket. He was chewing gum vigorously as they approached him.

"Hi, Virgil, have you seen this one yet?" Ruth asked.

Virgil gave her an appreciative look and cracked his gum. Ruth was better developed than Rosemary. What was more, Ruth's blonde hair was flashier than Rosemary's mousy brown. Rosemary couldn't help feeling a little jealous of Ruth, who could imitate Mae West to perfection with the kind of looks she had. She knew that was why Virgil had let Ruth in free at least three times earlier in the year, times when they had arranged to meet inside and Rosemary had already paid.

Virgil cracked his gum again and handed Ruth her ticket stub. "I ain't seen it yet," he said. "They don't have a private showing just for me. But I hear it's real romantic. You'll like it, kid. Kissin' and stuff—*you* know." He grinned, and Ruth giggled.

Rosemary walked past him stiffly and took her stub without saying anything.

Ruth nudged her. "I think he likes me," she whispered.

"For heaven's sake, you can do better than a bumpkin like that," Rosemary told her.

"You're just jealous," Ruth said calmly.

Rosemary bit back a retort. She did not want anything to spoil this moment. Certainly not Virgil with his pimply, chinless face. This was the time when the magic of the movies began to take hold, for they had now stepped upon the carpeted floor of the inner lobby, where more movie posters were scattered among comfortable sofas and Spanish-style architecture, and where even the drinking fountain was nestled in a pebble-lined inset in the wall. In the ladies' lounge huge blown-up color photographs of Carole Lombard, the late Jean Harlow, Clark Gable, and Spencer Tracy looked across the room at cream-colored dressing tables with large round mirrors above them and subdued indirect lighting that flattered the face.

Sometimes Rosemary thought that if she could just have this whole place to herself she wouldn't have to see the movie at all—it was so glamorous, so different from the outside world, which was still struggling out of the Depression. Here there was no unemployment, no dreary western Pennsylvania town smudged with soft-coal smoke. She could imagine herself famous and rich and beautiful—in short, a movie star.

She and Ruth primped in front of the mirrors for a few seconds, then left the ladies' room and entered the theater itself, which was decorated like a Spanish courtyard. From the ceiling stars winked from a sky of midnight blue. A few clouds rolled by. Nude figures, with their hands discreetly arranged, looked down at them from niches made to look like balconies, while below them in the boxes red velvet curtains moved in a breeze from somewhere in the theater's nether regions.

The girls snuggled down in front-row seats as the house lights dimmed and the curtain in front of the screen parted with a flourish. This early in the day they had the theater almost to themselves. As the seal of the Pennsylvania Board of Censors flashed upon the screen, Rosemary felt almost as if she were in her own screening room. Then, on the screen, a camera lens swung around at them proclaiming that it was the "eyes and ears of the world." The newsreel had begun.

In silence they ate the spearmint leaves they had bought at the five-and-ten before they came in, as hundreds of Hitler Youth goose-stepped before their eyes. They then watched as Hitler and Stalin, both of them smiling, signed a nonaggression pact.

"The war has started, you know," Rosemary whispered.

"Yeah, I know," said Ruth.

It seemed very far away, perhaps on another planet, that

the British were testing their gas masks and the French were saying that a line called Maginot would hold. It was all there in front of them, but it seemed less real than the movie they had come to see. After all, weren't they also showing on the screen a baseball game between the New York Yankees and the Chicago White Sox, a scene from the World's Fair in New York, and debutante Cobina Wright, Jr., at a party?

The newsreel ended, to be followed by a Mickey Mouse cartoon, an Our Gang comedy, a Pete Smith Special, and the previews of coming attractions. But the picture finally started. Suddenly they were transported back in time to a lonely, dark house on a moor. Suddenly, in the wind and the rain, there was a voice calling, "Heathcliff," and they were swept up by it all, outside themselves, each of them the tempestuous Catherine, wildly in love with the half-demon gypsy Heathcliff.

When it ended, tears were streaming down their cheeks; they could not speak. The newsreel had almost ended for the second time before Ruth said, "Wasn't it *wonderful.*"

"Yes," Rosemary breathed. She did not want to speak of it to Ruth. Even though she was her best friend, it seemed too precious. She had never seen such a movie. When I love, it will be like that, she decided.

They did not mention it, but they knew they were going to stay to see it again. When, at last, they staggered out of the theater, the day was well advanced toward evening.

"I'm going to go over and see if the library is open and get the book *Wuthering Heights,*" Rosemary said. "Want to come along?"

"I'd like to, but I can't," said Ruth. "I have to go home. My mother's going to be having fits 'cause I stayed so long." Calling out, "Gum-bye for now," she rushed off and left Rosemary to wend her way euphorically in the other direction.

With the spell of the movie still upon her, Rosemary no longer saw the ugliness of the town with its narrow streets, and she no longer smelled the stale peanut odor being puffed out through the open doors of the two five-and-tens or the damp yeastiness of the bars where men, still out of work, lounged and looked at her with vacant, bleak eyes. She passed them all, dreaming.

The library was still open, and the young librarian in charge had a copy of *Wuthering Heights* on her desk. "I knew someone would be sure to ask for it after the picture opened," she said with a grin. "How was the movie? Did you like it?"

"It was the most beautiful movie I've ever seen," said Rosemary.

"You'll like the book too," said the librarian. She stamped it out and handed it to her.

"Thank you." Rosemary clutched the book to her and hurried out. Outside, she opened it and started picking out passages she remembered from the film. As she floated home, she acted out the parts in her mind, seeing herself in the part of Cathy instead of Merle Oberon.

Of course she had always known she was going to be a movie star, but she was going to be a *great actress* as well. Already she felt more ethereal. Her usual springy walk was gone. She felt as if she were flowing along, as if her feet had no contact with the sidewalk.

When she reached home, Mrs. Hauser met her at the door, and Rosemary looked at her in a kind of daze.

"I've been waiting for you to get here, Rosemary," she said.

"Have you?"

"I hope you can come down tonight, at least for a few minutes. My nephew is going to be here."

"Your nephew?"

"Yes. Douglas. He just got back from a visit to California —Hollywood. I thought you'd like to meet him, knowing how interested you are in Hollywood and movies and all that."

"Oh, yes, sure," said Rosemary. She wanted to ask how old Mrs. Hauser's nephew was. Was he Rosemary's age? Was he five, fifty, or what? But she didn't want to appear too interested in a boy—that is, if he was one. Besides, it was always awkward when adults arranged things like that. She would rather bow out. But of course, there was no way to do it gracefully, so she said, "What time do you want me to come down?"

"Well, he'll be here for supper. Why don't you come down afterward?"

"All right," said Rosemary.

She forgot to close the stair door behind her and had to go back to do it. Then she dashed up the stairs two at a time.

"Mother, do I have to go down and meet Mrs. Hauser's nephew? Can't I get out of it?"

"I don't know how. After all, she thought she was doing

you a favor by asking you. It won't hurt you to go down and be friendly for a little while."

"How old is he?"

"I have no idea."

Rosemary sighed. "I had planned to listen to the 'Hit Parade' and read. I'm sure if he's Mrs. Hauser's nephew he'll be awful."

"Have you been at the movies all the live-long day again?"

"Uh-huh."

"Rosemary, I wish you wouldn't stay and see the pictures over. It's ridiculous sitting in a dark theater all day when you could be enjoying the sunshine."

"It was worth it," said Rosemary.

Rosemary had mixed feelings about the coming evening. She thought it would be exciting to talk to someone about Hollywood, someone who had actually been there, but how could she go up to a complete stranger and say, "Oh, by the way, I hear you've been to Hollywood. Do tell me about it"?

She tried not to worry about it, but instead, after the supper dishes were done, started reading her book. Inevitably, however, at eight o'clock Mrs. Hauser opened the door downstairs and called up, a trill in her voice, "Rosemary . . . why don't you come down for a little while?"

"Oh, dear," said Rosemary. She cast a beseeching look at her mother, who merely smiled. Dragging her feet, Rosemary went down the stairs.

When she got to the bottom, Mrs. Hauser called out, "We're in here, Rosemary."

Rosemary followed her voice to the living room. Mrs. Hauser and a strange lady were sitting on the sofa. Mr. Hauser was in his usual chair drinking a cup of coffee, Bingo at his feet. The radio was on, and some soprano was singing.

The boy had been sitting in the chair next to the radio. As Rosemary entered he got up, towering over her. He was about sixteen, with hazel eyes and sort of rumpled up curly auburn hair, and . . . *he looked like William Holden.*

Completely devastated, Rosemary stood there, as Heathcliff, the demon lover, disappeared from her mind and Mrs. Hauser's nephew began to take his place. Mrs. Hauser was introducing them, but words could not penetrate Rosemary's consciousness for the moment. Her breath seemed to have left her; she did not know what to say.

"Hello," he said, and his voice was even a lot like William Holden's. He smiled in uncertainty. He, too, seemed uncomfortable.

Embarrassed, they stood there looking at each other and then away. Rosemary swallowed. There must be something she could say.

"Why don't you tell her about Hollywood, Douglas? Rosemary is a real movie fan, aren't you, dear? Go out in the dining room and talk, where our conversation won't disturb you. Go ahead," said Mrs. Hauser, all smiles.

"Er—yeah. Sure," Douglas said. He followed Rosemary to the dining room, which was situated halfway between the hall in the front and the kitchen in the back, with Mr. and Mrs. Hauser's bedroom off to one side.

Rosemary hesitated, then, her legs shaking, dropped into a chair at the dining-room table. Douglas, a resigned look on his face, sat opposite her. Her heart was thudding with shyness and admiration, but she allowed herself a quick glance at him before concentrating firmly on the table-cloth. It was Mrs. Hauser's usual lace one, which was some-what worn at the places where it folded over the edge of the table.

"What do you want to know about Hollywood?" Doug-las asked. He glanced toward the living room as if toward a haven, so that Rosemary was uncomfortably aware that he would rather be anywhere but here. After all, he looked old enough to be a junior in high school. What possible interest could he have in a thirteen-year-old who was still in junior high? All at once she felt sorry for him. But she felt sorrier for herself. She could think of no graceful way to get either one of them out of this situation, and much as she wanted to know him better, she didn't relish being a burden to him, or giving the impression of being a movie-crazy little fool—even if that was what she was.

"I saw Grauman's Chinese Theater—where they have the footprints, you know," he began in desperation. "My mother and I passed Gary Cooper on the street, and we saw Alice Faye eating in a restaurant."

"Did they look the way they look in the movies?" Rose-mary asked dutifully.

"Oh, yes. Pretty much. Yes. Not as large, of course."

"I guess not." Silence flooded in and filled the conversational gap. Rosemary began again. "Did you visit any studios?"

"We were going to, but we were only there for two weeks and we didn't have time. We did go on a tour of the movie stars' homes."

"Oh?" said Rosemary. Ordinarily she would have welcomed this chance to learn about Hollywood. Instead it was a painful ordeal. "Which ones?" she asked.

Douglas thought for a moment. "Ah—Shirley Temple . . . Bing Crosby . . . ah . . ." He paused. "Haven't I seen you before? Have you always lived around here?"

"Oh, yes. But you're not, are you?"

"From around here? Yes, but not lately. I used to live on this street, up near Mountain Street, but we moved to West Virginia for a few years. Now we're back. We live right across the street—moved in the other day."

Rosemary had been nervously twisting the end of the tablecloth. She stopped. She didn't want to think what she was thinking. "Is your last name Mitchell?"

"It sure is."

"Then," she said in a somewhat strangled voice, "you must have a brother, one they used to call Mitch."

Puzzled, he shook his head. "I don't have any brother at all. Just a married sister who lives in Wheeling." He smiled. "They used to call *me* Mitch when I lived here before."

Rosemary's jaw dropped. She got up slowly. "I—er—" She backed away. Her cheeks felt fiery. She put her hands up to them, longing to cover her face entirely.

"What's the matter?" he said. "Did I say something wrong?"

47

He was so good-looking, so polite, and he *seemed* so nice. Yet he admitted to being that awful boy who had spanked her, who had humiliated her so. The old hatred for him began to rise in her chest, despite all her attempts to choke it back. After all, he couldn't have changed *that* much in such a short time. Underneath his handsome facade he must still have that same mean kid hidden somewhere, just as Rosemary's old self still existed deep down inside her.

"Nothing's the matter," she said, struggling to keep her voice even. "I have to go, that's all. I think I hear my mother calling me."

"I didn't hear anything," Douglas said. He was staring at her, his hand on her arm, as comprehension dawned. "Oh, for the love of Mike!" he said. "I remember you now. Aren't you that little kid who used to tag along after the boys, the one who came up to my house one day and tore into me in the garage?" He laughed, his eyes dancing with amusement.

"We had a—a disagreement," Rosemary said with all the dignity she could summon. "Don't you remember? You stole my cap pistol."

"Did I? I don't remember that." He laughed again. "I do remember I had to spank you. There wasn't much else I could do. You were so little, and you wanted to fight. What a little twerp!"

"I was just trying to get my cap pistol back," she said bitterly.

"Aw, come on! What difference does it make now?"

"It just wasn't fair," she insisted. But she was thinking, The cap pistol *doesn't* matter now! Why are we talking about it? What bothered her was the humiliation he caused. But then he'd never understand that.

"You mean you've been carrying a grudge all this time?" There was incomprehension on Douglas's face, then a kind of disgust, and for a minute he did look just like the little boy Mitch she remembered.

"I guess I have," she said. Trying to act self-assured, she walked to the door, but since he couldn't possibly comprehend how she felt, she knew he probably thought she was crazy. "Thanks for telling me about Hollywood," she said. As she backed out of the room her voice suddenly trailed off.

"You're welcome," Douglas said sharply.

"Going already?" said Mrs. Hauser, coming up behind Rosemary. "I thought you two would have such a lot to talk about."

"Oh, yes, we have," Rosemary said, her voice too high. She turned to Mrs. Hauser, realized she was wringing her hands, and jerkily dropped them to her sides. "We had a nice talk," she said. "Thank you for inviting me."

At the stairway she sneaked a look back into the dining room. Douglas had disappeared. He had apparently seized this chance to escape into the kitchen.

Rosemary herself hurried back upstairs with a sense of profound relief. She couldn't have borne staying in the same room with him a moment longer. Oh, if only, before she came down here this evening, she had had some warning about who Douglas really was! If only she had been prepared. As it was, she had a horrid feeling she had made a terrible mess of things.

Dear Daddy,

I hope you get this. I am going to send it to the hotel in Minneapolis. Do you like traveling around the country? I would. Maybe next time I can go along with you. I would be good as a girl singer. Ruth says she would be better, but then she is always saying she can do things better than me. That doesn't make it so!

School has started, of course, and it's going along pretty well now. I am in the Dramatic Club, the Writing Club, and the Chorus, and am on the school paper, *The Green and the Gold.* I was also in the Camera Club, but I gave it up because I didn't have a camera.

The noon hour dances have started again too, and I can jitterbug as well as anybody now. Ruth's and my favorite record is "In the Mood" by Glenn Miller. It is fun to dance to. Only the trouble is, the girls dance with the girls, and the boys just watch and giggle. I have never danced with a boy.

Ginger Oppenheimer is going to have a cootie party next week. Have you ever played cootie? Ginger learned it from her cousin in Pittsburgh, and it's played at a table with one die. The numbers you throw on the die stand for the different parts of a bug that you draw, like his head, body, feelers, and so forth. It sounds pretty dumb to me, but Ginger says that once you start playing the game, it's like eating peanuts—you can't stop.

I just finished an infatuating book called *Wuthering Heights.* Ruth and I saw the movie also. It was wonderful. You should see it if you get a chance.

I guess Mother told you about Thompson. He is an irritating cat, and very fasstidious (sp?) too. His bathroom is in my bedroom (where else?) and he likes to have his pan kept very clean. He himself is very sloppy, though, and he scratches and kicks the dirt in all directions as if he's mad about something. Then I have to sweep it up.

I took Thompson to the vet too, to make sure he is healthy, and while he was there he bit him. (That is, Thompson bit the vet, not the other way around. Ha, ha.) Thompson always bites when he can't get his own way—for instance, if I don't feed him as fast as he thinks I should. He has bit me on the ankle several times. Mother says they are love bites, but they don't feel loving to me!

I have to go now. Mother says she will write the next time. She likes her new job, but she is very busy.

When are you coming home?

> *Your loving daughter,*
> *Rosemary*

P. S. Gramma is making me a Pierrette costume for the Halloween party at school.

The first issue of the school paper, *The Green and the Gold,* came out late in September. A week later, the staff of the paper was sitting around a classroom after school planning the next issue when Franny Stapleton, who was sitting at the teacher's desk as befitted her position as editor, turned to Rosemary and said, "Hey, I have an idea! How about me doing an article about you and Thompson?"

Rosemary had been woolgathering; now she gave a start. "What? I don't know what you mean."

"Yes, you do. Ruth told me about your new cat and how he has all that money."

Rosemary cast a reproachful look in Ruth's direction. Ruth quickly opened her social science book as if she had just at that moment decided to read tomorrow's assignment. "Some friend," Rosemary muttered.

"Aw, come on, Rosemary," Franny wheedled, "be a good sport. I could interview him. I could ask him questions like, Do you really have nine lives? It'd be a wonderful story."

Rosemary knew Franny was capable of doing the story anyway, in which case there was no telling what she might say. If she, Rosemary, went along with the idea, the story might at least be kinder.

"Please, Rosemary," Franny was saying, "let me go home with you and meet him. The cat's out of the bag now, anyway." She laughed.

"He sure is," Rosemary said. She shrugged. "Oh, all right. Why not? You might as well," she said.

By the time the meeting was over, Rosemary felt resigned to the inevitable. If she had to submit to an interview, she might as well be pleasant about it.

When she got home, however, she was totally unprepared to find her mother already there and looking somewhat frazzled. "Rosemary!" she said. "Thompson's been gone all day. I've looked everywhere for him. No one's seen him."

"Oh, Mother! How *could* you let him out?"

"I didn't 'let' him out, Rosemary. He must have got out. You know how he's been trying to. He wasn't here when I came home to lunch. I looked high and low for him. I've been so worried all afternoon that I couldn't keep my mind on my work. Finally, I got permission to come home early. But there's still no sign of him."

Rosemary flung her books on the coffee table. "What are we going to do now? Did Mrs. Hauser see him?"

"No."

"Let's go outside and look for him," said Franny sympathetically. "Maybe he's been asleep somewhere all day. My cat curls up under the porch and stays there for hours. Come on, Rosemary."

When they were back outside, Franny said, "You go one way and I'll go the other."

Rosemary nodded in agreement. She walked around to the back of the house, calling "Kitty, kitty, kitty" as she went. She could hear Franny doing the same thing out front. Rosemary had no hope, though. Thompson was diabolical. He hated them, and he would never come back. He *knew* how important he was.

For over half an hour they searched, up the street and down. Once a cat did come off a porch at Rosemary's calls, but it was a friendly little tiger cat, not an irritable-looking black-and-white one. Just as she turned to go back home she saw something that color lying in the middle of the street and her breath stopped, but closer inspection revealed it to be an old newspaper.

Back at the house she found Franny sitting on the steps. As Rosemary approached, she shook her head. Shoulders slumping, Rosemary sat down beside her.

"Is it really true," Franny asked, "that he's worth a thousand dollars?"

"Was," Rosemary groaned.

"Gosh, Rosemary, I'm sorry."

"Don't be. Nothing's really changed."

"Well, I'm sorry, all the same." Franny had been gazing across the street, and now, ever so slightly, her expression grew brighter. Rosemary looked hopefully in the same direction and saw Mitch—that is, Douglas—arriving home from school. Rosemary's heartbeat quickened. She hadn't talked to Douglas since that one unfortunate evening. She had *seen* him, from a distance, of course, from behind the curtains of the second floor, and she had *heard* him and his friends, who had gotten up a little jazz band, practicing in the front room of her—the Mitchell—house. She was certainly conscious of Douglas. She was also terrified of him, terrified of having him notice her, terrified of saying something silly and having him look at her in contempt. And so she always went out of her way to avoid him, even if it meant walking extra blocks or hiding behind the front door until he was gone.

And now Franny was saying, "Hey, maybe that boy has seen him."

Before Rosemary could stop her, Franny was crossing

the street in a long-legged stride, her fair pageboy hairdo bobbing. "Hi! Wait a minute! Could I ask you something?"

Douglas stopped and looked at her curiously.

"Have you seen a cat, a black-and-white cat?"

"No," said Douglas. "Have you lost one?"

"I haven't. But Rosemary has."

Douglas glanced over at Rosemary. From this distance she could not be sure what that look contained, and she felt she'd rather not find out. She was intensely aware of him, though. "I'm afraid I haven't seen any cat," he said. "I just this minute got home. If I do see him, I'll grab him."

"Forget it, Franny," Rosemary called. "He's lost. There's nothing we can do about it."

Franny smiled at Douglas, then turned and crossed back over to Rosemary. Douglas went into the house.

"He's cute," Franny said, her voice low.

"Um," said Rosemary.

She was glad when her mother appeared at the front door. "You know, it just occurred to me," she said, "that maybe Thompson will come if I clatter the dishes."

"What do you mean?"

He always comes to the kitchen when he hears the dishes rattling, because he hopes he'll get something to eat. Maybe, wherever he is, he'll hear it if I do that now."

Franny giggled. "Why don't you try it?" she said.

They followed Anne Beedy back up to the kitchen. She took two dessert dishes out of the cupboard, stood next to the window, and clattered them together. Then she banged a fork on top of one of them. "Here, kitty, kitty, kitty," she called.

The girls yelled out the window. "Here, kitty, kitty."
Anne banged the fork again.

"Sh!" said Franny. They all stopped and listened.

From somewhere, far, far away, they heard a faint cry.

"He's in the house!" Rosemary exclaimed.

They went out into the hallway, calling and listening alternately. The cry was repeated, more insistently this time. It was coming from Rosemary's room.

The three of them tiptoed up to the door. Everything was still now, and Anne rattled the fork again.

Rosemary started to go toward the closet, but then she noticed that the closet door was already slightly open. He wasn't in there.

"Mer-ow-er!" said Thompson. He sounded muffled—and annoyed.

"He's in the drawer!" Franny leaped toward the dresser and pulled open the large wide bottom drawer where Rosemary kept her sweaters and shirts. Thompson leaped out, his fur ruffled, his eyes stark with fury. He dashed past Rosemary and fled down the hall, his tail straight up in the air. Behind him, where he had been lying, he left a mass of black and white hairs plastered to Rosemary's pale-blue cardigan.

Anne Beedy sat down on the bed and laughed until she cried. Wiping her eyes, she said, "He must have been there ever since you got dressed this morning, Rosemary. How did you miss seeing him when you shut the drawer?"

"I was in a hurry," Rosemary told her. She stared in the direction Thompson had gone. "He didn't have to be so huffy about it. It was his own fault."

Franny put her jacket back on and prepared to go home. "Well, I guess I got my story," she said with an air of self-satisfaction. "And I know just how I'm going to write it."

With a sinking heart, Rosemary guessed she did.

Rosemary Beedy, world-renowned dancer, arrived at the party in her black-and-white Pierrette costume, made by the famous costume designer Irene. The costume, with its short flared skirt, showed off to perfection her slim graceful body and beautiful long dancer's legs, used to performing before the crowned heads of Europe. Her hair, tightly curled for the occasion, was fastened high on the back of her head so that it rippled down beguilingly toward her deliciously curved neck. As she entered the room and threw off her fur wrap, the dark, handsome King of Ruritania stared at her intently from a doorway, then whispered in a low, slightly accented voice, "Would you waltz with me, mademoiselle?"

Rosemary's arms and legs were cold. What could her grandmother, who always worried about drafts, have been thinking of when she had suggested making this costume? It was becoming, yes, but also decidedly skimpy. Rosemary always wore a cardigan to school over her white shirt, and a warm skirt below that. She had never realized before how drafty were the halls and gymnasium of Lincoln Junior High School.

Everybody had told her she looked perfectly lovely: her grandmother, her mother, Mr. and Mrs. Hauser, Malvina, and her Aunt Jo, her father's youngest sister, who had come to dinner that night. And Rosemary had felt lovely

—there in the warmth of the house, but even all these people could not warm up the gym, where cold breezes seemed to come from all directions.

"Rosemary," Ruth said as they danced a foxtrot together, "you have goose bumps all over your arms."

"My legs too," Rosemary told her. "I'm freezing."

"Why don't you go put your coat on?"

"I suppose I'll have to," Rosemary said, thinking how awful *that* was going to look, her old lumpy, brick-red coat on the dance floor. Not that it mattered, she supposed; she had already spent the first part of the evening dancing with Ruth.

Ruth, she thought, looked positively smug, even though her costume was not what she had planned it to be. Because of her alleged resemblance to Mae West, Ruth had written the star a letter asking if she would send her some of her old clothes, but Mae West had not seen fit to answer her. Therefore, Ruth had been reduced at the last minute to assembling a costume out of her mother's cast-off clothing. The result was a red-and-purple gypsy dress, with long sleeves and a long skirt, and a bright kerchief hiding her yellow hair. Earrings dangled below the edge of the kerchief. She looked marvelous, and knew it—and, what was more, she was warm.

Ruth stared over Rosemary's shoulder and said, "Malcolm Gurney's coming this way. He looks as if he's going to ask you to dance."

Rosemary's heart gave a little flip. Not that Malcolm was so much; he was shorter than she was, and sometimes he smelled as if he hadn't taken a bath. Still, he was a boy, and boys hardly ever asked anyone to dance.

Malcolm was close to them now. Like most of the boys, he hadn't bothered to put together a costume, but he had bought a mask at the five-and-ten which was now pushed up over his head. "Hey, Ruth," he said, "how about it?"

Ruth looked surprised. "Sure," she said.

Rosemary quickly retreated. "I've got to get my coat," she muttered. She fled to the classroom, grabbed her coat out of the closet, and stood huddled by the radiator. Well, she hadn't wanted to dance with short old Malcolm anyway.

Or had she? She sighed. Of course she had. She wanted to dance and be popular just like any other girl, except that when chances came, she longed to back off. Why, she was almost as scared of Malcolm as she was of—well, Douglas. In the past year or so, boys had begun to seem so mysterious. . . .

Oh, she would never be poised and at ease like some girls she knew—even Ruth, it seemed. It was just too much to hope for. And she would probably always wear the wrong thing wherever she went. She looked down at herself. Her coat had fallen open over one of her bare legs. The leg looked blue. Oh, how could she ever have thought she looked pretty?

Ruth came into the classroom, her skirt and scarves swirling. "They're going to serve refreshments. Come on. We'll go load up our plates and then come back here and eat with some of the other girls."

Rosemary hated to go back to the gym looking like this, but not to go would seem odd and unsporting, so she said, "OK," and followed Ruth out.

"I'm having a wonderful time," Ruth said. "Aren't you?"

"Oh, yes," said Rosemary, and she tried to sound as enthusiastic about it as Ruth had.

And she did have fun after she and her friends brought their plates back to the schoolroom. Some boys drifted in, too, and they all told jokes and laughed a lot. None of them ever did go back and dance.

Still, that night as she lay in bed thinking it over, Rosemary decided that coed parties were torture. It would be different in the future. When she had succeeded as an actress and had married William Holden, they would come back here on a visit and go to a dance at the gym, and people would be so impressed that everyone would want to dance with her. . . . Half asleep, she smiled, and it didn't strike her as a bit peculiar that while, in her dream, she had grown up and had improved both in looks and in poise, Ruth and Malcolm and all the rest were still thirteen and fourteen.

7

One Sunday morning Rosemary awoke to the sound of rain falling on the pavement in the narrow passage between the Hauser house and the one next door. Her ordinarily dark room was darker than usual, and she was in a cramped position on one side of the mattress, to which Thompson had managed to crowd her while taking for himself the precise middle of the small bed. He was curled up in a tight ball, his nose hidden beneath his tail. Rosemary slid her legs under him until he rolled over and landed in an undignified heap on the floor. The place where he had lain felt warm and cozy.

"Rosemary." Her mother stuck her head inside the door. She was already dressed and had her coat on. "Oh," she said, "you're awake."

"How could I help it, with this monster taking up the whole bed?"

"Why did you let him do it? You should have pushed him off."

"I didn't know he was doing it; I was asleep."

"Well, I'm sorry. You'll have to be firmer with him." Her mother changed the subject. "You don't mind going to Sunday school alone today, do you? I'm going to Mass at St. Anthony's with Marie." Marie was one of her mother's closest friends.

"OK," said Rosemary. "Are we going to Gramma's for dinner?"

Her mother looked resigned. "They expect it."

"OK," said Rosemary again. "I'll meet you there." She rolled out of bed.

Rosemary got dressed, had a glass of milk with Cocomalt in it, fed Thompson, changed his pan, and dutifully went on to Sunday school at the Lutheran church on Wallace Boulevard. Afterward, it was still short of eleven o'clock, and too early to meet her mother, so she decided to go back home to read for fifteen minutes or so. The rain had become heavy and the sky was very dark. But she preferred it that way; she preferred Sunday to be dreary. Perhaps it was because sunshine mocked you on Sunday; there were so many indoor things you had to do before you were free. You had to go to Sunday school and perhaps church, and then there was that long, leaden midday meal that left everybody sitting around feeling heavy and sleepy and trying not to belch. Another reason she disliked Sunday was because all the movie theaters were closed. A day in which it wasn't even *possible* to go the movies depressed Rosemary no end.

The house was quiet when Rosemary returned from Sunday school. The Hausers had gone to their married daughter's for dinner. Nevertheless, the smell of pot roast met her nostrils as she opened the door to the stairs. Malvina, as usual, was cooking dinner on her hot plate for her boyfriend Arthur. No. *Boyfriend* wasn't the right word for him. He was a grown-up man, even though he did still live with his mother. Rosemary had heard Mrs. Hauser whispering about it to her own mother. His mother was an invalid, and Arthur couldn't afford to support both her and Malvina, so he continued to live with his mother, only coming to see Malvina on Sunday. Unlike Rosemary, Malvina must live all week in anticipation of Sunday. On that day she had a man of her own to cook for.

Malvina even saw Arthur on those Sundays when he had to work. Arthur was a conductor on a streetcar that traversed the countryside between Lynnfield and a nearby town. When he had to work on Sunday, Malvina went with him, riding back and forth on the streetcar all day.

She had her happy Sunday face on now, as she stepped out of her room. "Arthur?" she called.

"No, it's me," said Rosemary. "Your dinner smells good."

"Thanks. I hope it tastes good too." Malvina looked about her. "How's Thompson? I haven't seen him today."

"He's probably sleeping. You know, he's an awful cat. I don't believe he likes Mother and me at all. And he hates living here, after having a whole house to run around in."

Malvina laughed. "He can always visit me, Rosemary. I like cats."

"I'm glad you do," Rosemary said. She waved and went into the living room to read.

A little later she heard Arthur come in and heard Malvina reminding him to shut the door to the stairway so Thompson wouldn't get out. Then they went into her room and closed the door upon their private world, where Arthur feasted on the one meal of the week he didn't have to cook himself, and Malvina had what was probably her one nourishing meal of the week.

At eleven thirty Rosemary started off. By now the rain was coming down in streams and the wind had picked up. It whipped under her umbrella and set it to flapping, so that Rosemary felt spray on her face. But she enjoyed wild weather. It made her think of a Brontë novel.

When she reached the Wakely house the trees were shaking in the storm and scattering rain-battered leaves on the overgrown driveway. Somewhere a door creaked on a broken hinge. Near the road a branch rubbing against another made a sound like the cry of a newborn baby.

Rosemary shivered and walked a little faster, and soon tall trees hid the Wakely house from view. Then, a bit of a way past it, Rosemary's grandparents' little house appeared, with its neat postage-stamp lawn inside the picket fence shiny with rain, and her grandfather's Ford parked in front of the gate.

When she opened the door the rooms were steamy with cooking, and Rosemary made her way to the large kitchen, where her grandmother was standing at the stove.

"Chicken and dumplings, right?" said Rosemary, going over to the pot and sniffing.

"How did you guess?" said her grandmother.

Rosemary smiled. Her grandmother *always* had chicken on Sunday.

Her grandfather came in through the back door, carrying a pan of Brussels sprouts from his little garden. He kissed Rosemary on the top of her head. "Hi, punkin. How are you?" Without waiting for an answer, he held out the Brussels sprouts. "Aren't they little beauties?" he said. "And a little cold weather only makes them better."

Rosemary lifted the lid of the jam pot and dipped her finger into it. "You're a wonderful gardener. That helps too," she said.

Her grandfather nodded at the compliment. "What marvelous movie did you see yesterday?" he asked. Unlike most people, he really acted interested in the things that interested her.

"*Beau Geste*, with Gary Cooper and Ray Milland," Rosemary told him. She sat down next to him and proceeded to describe the movie in great detail, and with gestures. Along with interruptions from her grandmother and the arrival of her mother, her acting out of the movie filled the time until dinner.

Later, after dinner, the three women of the family did the dishes while Grampa, looking stuffed, sat in his rocker beside the steamed-up window. "I may never eat again," he said. He patted his round stomach, the only outward physical evidence of his wife's hobby, and belched softly.

"Yes, you will," his wife told him confidently, her arms deep in soap suds. "Around three o'clock you'll be asking me what's in the refrigerator."

Rosemary knew that to be true. If there was anything predictable in life, it was the routine of her grandparents' Sundays. After the dishes were done, they would all sit around the kitchen table playing cards. Then they would have a snack and play some more cards. Then they would have supper and listen to Jack Benny. Stultifying, she thought, dreading the long afternoon that lay ahead of her.

But as if in answer to her thought, at just that moment, someone rang the doorbell, which made a kind of rasping jangle.

"I'll get it!" said Rosemary.

Even before she got to the door she could see who was standing outside on the porch shaking her umbrella. It was Ruth.

"Hi," she said. "What are you doing?"

Rosemary wrinkled up her nose. "Drying dishes."

"Bore-bore," said Ruth. "What else is new?" Then, as the others waved to her from the kitchen, she called out, "Hi, Mr. and Mrs. Nicholas. Hi, Mrs. Beedy." She lowered her voice again. "Can you come over? I'm dying of boredom. My father fell asleep over the paper; my mother went upstairs for a nap; and my brother went someplace with his girl. The house is a tomb. But if you came over, we could play Monopoly or something."

"Wouldn't we wake everybody up?"

"Nah. We could go out in the clubhouse. It isn't too cold for that."

The "clubhouse" was an old chicken coop behind Ruth's house that the two girls had one day laboriously cleaned out for their own use. To Rosemary it still smelled of chickens, but anything was preferable to the usual Sunday ritual. "Sure," she said. "Let's go."

A few minutes later she was running down the road with

Ruth in the rain. "You saved my life," she said. "Don't you just *hate* Sunday?"

"It's a prison!" said Ruth, and she slopped through a puddle in her floppy galoshes. "I wish there was something exciting to do."

"I thought you wanted to play Monopoly."

"Oh, I don't know," said Ruth. "I'd like to do something different, something we've never done before, wouldn't you?"

"But what?" Rosemary asked.

They had reached the corner. Beyond stood the Wakely house behind its stone wall and the veil of rain.

"Hey," said Ruth softly. "Hey . . . I just got an idea. Let's explore the Wakely house." She turned and looked at Rosemary through eyes bright with mischief. "Have you ever been inside?"

"No-o. . . ."

"Let's go then."

"Oh, I don't think we'd better."

"Why not? You're not scared, are you, because it's haunted?"

They were standing by the gate now, and it was firmly padlocked. "No, I'm not scared—except that we might get caught. Anyway, we can't get in."

Ruth gave her a look of contempt. "You're just making excuses. No one is going to see us. No one would even care. We'll climb a tree and get over the wall that way." Ruth closed her umbrella and gave it a toss. It landed on top of the wall. She wasn't long in following it as she scrambled up a sycamore growing nearby. Ruth stepped out of the tree onto the wall and retrieved her umbrella. Opening it and holding it over her head, she did a little dance.

"Are you coming or not?" she asked.

"Oh, all right," Rosemary said, curiosity winning over caution, and she, too, went up the tree.

They walked along on top of the wall until they came to another tree, one they could climb down, and then they were on the grounds of the Wakely house at last. They were standing near the swimming pool, which now had a few rain puddles in it. Grass grew up through the cracks.

Ruth led the way around the pool. "It must have been nice here once," she observed. She turned and grinned at Rosemary. "Now the place looks like something Dracula might rent."

"Ru-uth . . . !"

"Oh, phooey, he'd be asleep at this time of day, anyway."

Across the lawn, which was deep in weeds, Ruth led the way. She stepped onto the terrace where shaggy rose-bushes, bent over by the rain and by the weight of their dead blossoms, dripped rotting petals onto the flagstones. Ruth was busily jabbering. "We've got to find a way in," she was saying, as she peered through one of the French windows that opened onto the terrace. "There's a big room in there. But the door's locked," she added, turning the knob and pushing. "Come on," she said, and she started around the side of the house.

Now that Rosemary was close to the house, it seemed like a living presence, hulking and huge. She felt intimidated and small, as if she might be swallowed up by it and never see the light of day again. She did not want to go in—and yet she did—and so she followed Ruth nervously, her wet shoes making squishing sounds in the undergrowth.

At a side door Ruth stopped. "Look! The window on this door is broken. I'll bet someone already broke in. It's unlocked too!" she cried.

"Funny," said Rosemary in a shaky voice. She stood back, ready to run, as Ruth pushed the door in and stood looking up a short stairway into the dark interior of the Wakely house.

But now even Ruth seemed reluctant to enter, and she stood there hesitating.

Rosemary whispered, "Let's go home."

"No," said Ruth. She took Rosemary's hand and drew her into the house.

To the left, stairs went down into the damp darkness of the cellar, but directly in front of them the little stairway led toward another door, which was ajar. Rosemary kept close to Ruth as they went up and pushed it open all the way. They stepped into a hallway. To the right they could make out the outlines of a kitchen, so they went left and came out underneath a staircase in an enormous hallway. The staircase went up and up, past the second floor, past the third floor, to the tower in the roof. Rosemary had never seen such a staircase; it seemed to soar.

So Ruth's story was true! The staircase *was* here. Maybe the blood was, too, the blood where Aurora had braced herself against the wall on her way down.

"Isn't it beautiful!" said Ruth. "Let's go all the way to the very top. We can look out the window in the tower."

Rosemary kept taking deep breaths. She was scared, but

at the same time, now that she was here, she longed to explore the house and walk up and down that fairy-tale staircase. She remained close to Ruth's heels as they started up it.

"You know what?" Ruth said in an awed voice. "I think this wallpaper is made of *satin.*" She ran her hand along it as they wound their way upward.

Ruth stopped so suddenly that Rosemary bumped into her. "Rosemary," Ruth whispered. Her voice sounded shaky. "Look." She stepped to one side, holding on to the banister, so Rosemary could see what she had seen.

There, in a few places, about halfway between the first and second floors, the lattices of fading flowers in the satin wallpaper were marred by brown stains.

"Blood," Ruth breathed.

"Oh, no!" Rosemary didn't want it to be blood. "It—it could be rust."

"How would rust get here?" Ruth asked her ominously. "Besides," she added, "look at the steps."

Where they were standing the carpet treads were missing on several of the steps.

Ruth shook her head. "The carpet must have been a mess," she said.

"Oh, Ruth!" Rosemary put her hands up to her mouth. She didn't know whether she was going to be sick, or cry, or both. She had only half believed the tale before, but to find that every detail in it was true was almost more than she could bear. A human being, a girl like herself, had really had her life taken from her on this very spot, taken long before it should have ended, and it had been taken violently. The violence must have remained in the house—why, she could feel it all around her.

"Let's get out of here," she said, her voice barely audible.

"Oh, for heaven's sake," Ruth said. "It happened a long time ago. It must be at least ten years."

"I don't care; I don't like it," said Rosemary. Above her the stairway seemed to circle around and around like a corkscrew, without ever coming to an end. She felt as if she could hear someone screaming, screaming. . . .

The next thing she knew she was running down the stairs.

"Rosemary, come back. It isn't true," Ruth shouted. "I made it all up."

But Rosemary didn't believe Ruth now, and even if she had made the story up, it had all become true in some mysterious way, as if the two of them had made it so vivid to themselves that they had willed it into being. And so she continued in her flight out of the house and across the overgrown grounds to the place where they had climbed in. She clambered up the tree and jumped down off the wall, landing on all fours.

Ruth was right behind her. Before jumping off the wall she threw down the two umbrellas. "You left your umbrella behind," she said. She jumped down and landed beside Rosemary. "Why did you run away like that?" she said accusingly. "You scared me half to death. Did you see something? A ghost?"

"No, but I might have—any minute."

"Baloney!" said Ruth. "Come on back." Then, when Rosemary didn't respond, she added, "Well, *I'm* going back. I want to see the whole house, even if you don't." She turned around and climbed back up the tree. From the top of the wall she stood surveying Rosemary, hands on hips. "Are you coming?"

"No," said Rosemary calmly. "I'm going home. See you." She picked up her umbrella, raised it over her head, and marched off.

She had gone about two blocks when she heard someone running behind her. "Hey, wait up," Ruth yelled.

Rosemary waited, carefully hiding a mild feeling of satisfaction. Usually she was the one who gave in on things, Ruth being the more stubborn one. "I thought you wanted to look at the house some more," she said when Ruth caught up with her.

"I did want to," Ruth said, "but it's no fun doing it by myself. You're such a killjoy, Rosemary."

"Sorry. But it was your story that scared me."

Ruth grinned. "You have to admit, though, it was pretty good. I even believed it myself for a while there."

Rosemary smiled back. She felt safe now and had no hard feelings. "Want to come down to my house and read movie magazines?" she asked. "It'll be more comfortable than the chicken coop—I mean the clubhouse."

"Good idea," Ruth agreed. "But first I've got to stop and put on some dry clothes. The way it's been blowing, my skirt's all wet, and I hate the way it feels."

"I know. Me too," said Rosemary. "Come on down when you've changed. I'll go ahead."

"OK," Ruth said, and when they reached her house, she called out "Gum-bye," and ran up the steps.

Rosemary proceeded on alone. By now she realized that the rain had stopped, at least for the time being, and so she closed her umbrella. Ahead of her a boy of about ten came running out of his house with a football under his arm. He was a happy-looking boy with a face full of freckles that blended into one another.

"Hi, Danny," said Rosemary. "It's going to rain some more, you know."

"I don't care," he answered cheerfully. He kicked the ball into the vacant lot next door—the same lot where, a long time ago, Mitch and his friends had played. "Want to kick a few?" he yelled as he ran after the ball.

"Oh, I don't think so," she said, and she started to walk on. The three years' difference between her age and Danny's yawned like an abyss, and she was afraid someone might see her playing with him. Then, for some reason, it occurred to her suddenly that three years was also the difference between her age and Douglas's—not that that mattered. Yet she hesitated. After all, Danny was probably deep in the Sunday doldrums too, and had no one to play with. "Oh, all right," she said. "Why not?" She took off her jacket and leaned her umbrella against a tree. She ran into the field a little way. "See if you can kick it toward me," she said.

The lot was full of mud holes. Rosemary found it hard to avoid them as she held out her arms for the football, but she caught it all right, even though it muddied the front of her dress a little.

She positioned the ball in front of her, dropped it, and managed to kick it before it landed. It soared across the field, hitting Danny so hard in his midsection that he sat down with a grunt. "Hey, you're good," he said.

"So are you," Rosemary told him generously. She watched as he kicked the football back to her, but this time she was not so lucky in catching it. The ball landed in a puddle close enough to her to splash her legs and dapple the hem of her dress with mud.

"Kick it back," Danny called.

"OK." Rosemary picked up the drippy ball. Again she carefully positioned it and gave it a good strong kick. The ball sailed into the air, higher and higher. Watching it, Rosemary felt pretty proud of herself. The ball curved and began to come down. Danny ran around the lot trying to figure out where it would land. Its descent was swift now, and Rosemary could see that it was going to drop straight into a large puddle near the sidewalk. Simultaneously she saw a figure coming down that sidewalk, a figure who was going to reach the side of the puddle at the same time the ball landed. The figure was walking with great self-confidence, head high, thoughts obviously miles away.

"Watch out!" Rosemary shrieked.

The figure looked toward her curiously, but did not stop. Like fate the ball descended. When it hit the puddle, black water arched up and skimmed out in all directions. *Now* the figure stopped.

In horror Rosemary just stood there. "I'm so sor—!" She cut herself short, realizing that she was looking into the cold eyes of Douglas Mitchell.

He was wearing a light-tan raincoat, a *new* raincoat—

anyone could see that—it might even be the first time he had it on. But now the front of that raincoat was covered with black muddy water that dripped down over it and onto his shoes.

Rosemary swallowed. "Please," she said, not knowing what else to say. "I am sorry." She fumbled for words. "I'll have it cleaned for you. . . . Forgive me. . . . I didn't know the ball would land there . . . or that anyone was coming down the street. . . . Honest, I—" Hardly aware of what she was doing in her embarrassment, she grabbed the sleeve of the coat as if she wanted, right then and there, to run off with it to the dry cleaner.

"Don't bother," he said, pulling away, and she hoped he didn't notice, at least not just then, that where her hand had been, wet, muddy fingerprints remained. "Please don't bother. I'll take care of it," he said. "It's nothing. It was an accident." His words implied forgiveness, but his tone did not. She could tell he was disconcerted, perhaps even furious. His face was red. He took out his handkerchief and dabbed ineffectually at the mud on the front of his coat, and she knew, by the way he did it, that he had *liked* that coat, had felt that he looked nice in it. "It can be cleaned," he said, too forcefully.

"Yes," she said, choking back a sob, "and I'll pay for it. Let me know how much it is. I insist."

"Maybe," he said. He backed away from her a little bit, as if he were afraid of what she might do next, and for the first time she became aware of how she must look to him. Her dress, legs, and hands were covered with mud; her shoes were wet and muddy; her face felt hot from running; and she knew her hair was a mess. Now it was her turn to back away. She could not meet his eyes.

"Anyway, I am sorry," she mumbled.

"Thanks," he said inanely. He gave a sort of nod and then very quickly walked away from her.

Subdued, Rosemary watched him go; then, her shoulders slumping, she went over to the puddle and picked up the ball, hardly caring that it dripped more mud on her.

Danny, who had stayed back during her exchange with Douglas, now came and took it from her. "He was mad, wasn't he?"

She nodded. "I'm afraid so. But don't worry. It wasn't your fault." She picked up her jacket and her umbrella. It was starting to rain again, a little bit. She turned toward home, her feet leaving muddy tracks on the sidewalk for several steps. Danny walked with her. "Boys worry about how they look," she said, as much to herself as to him. "Someday you will too."

Danny shook his head. He doubted it. "But don't girls care? I'm glad you don't, Rosemary. You're fun."

Rosemary laughed ruefully. "I care," she said, "even if I do put my foot in my mouth sometimes."

He gazed at her with admiration. "That's hard to do."

"You'd be surprised how easy it is," she told him.

*M*r. Smith Goes to Washington, with Jimmy Stewart, was starting at the Lynnfield Palace, but Rosemary gritted her teeth and decided she would have to miss her movie that week, and maybe the following week too. She did not know how much it would cost to take Douglas's coat to be dry-cleaned; she knew only that she had to do it. She hated the idea of confronting him again, but Saturday morning she forced herself to march across the street to his house.

The November day was cold, but even with all the windows closed, she could hear what was going on inside— some sort of jam session, with a piano, drums, and saxophone. The "band" was so loud that she was sure no one would hear her when she rang the doorbell, but after a time Douglas's mother came down the hall from the kitchen.

Rosemary's heart was in her throat. "Could I see Douglas for a minute?" she whispered.

"What?" said Mrs. Mitchell, straining to hear her. "Douglas," she called, "be quiet for a minute, will you?"

The music stopped abruptly. Silence flowed out of the living room.

"Now what was it you were saying?" Mrs. Mitchell asked Rosemary.

"I—I—" said Rosemary. "I just wanted to ask Douglas something. Could I?"

"Why, of course," his mother told her. "Go right in. He's in the living room, as you must have heard. Doug, Rosemary Beedy's here to see you." Her smile was polite and pleasant as she held open the door, but Rosemary had the feeling that Mrs. Mitchell probably thought she was chasing Douglas.

That's not true, Rosemary mouthed to the woman's retreating back. I detest him. Then she sidled over to the archway between the hall and living room. She felt a shock when she looked in. She had half expected it to be the way it was when she and her parents had lived here. But of course that was silly; it had the Mitchells' furniture in it now, including a big upright piano. Hambone O'Reilly, an old friend of Douglas from the next street over, was sitting at the piano. He grinned at her.

She did not know the boy with the saxophone, who was standing a little behind Douglas, but when he saw Rosemary, he gave a sort of whining toot on the horn, and Rosemary was suddenly reminded of that other time in the garage. There was an uncomfortable similarity between then and now: she the only girl, an outsider; the boys with their bold stares.

She shifted her feet uneasily and tried to ignore the others. Her eyes were on Douglas, who was sitting behind the drums. He beat a soft tattoo on them and looked at her without much interest. "Hi," he said.

Rosemary struggled to keep her voice steady. "I'm sorry to bother you when you're practicing," she said. "I just wanted to ask you something, Douglas. What about your raincoat? How much was the cleaning bill? I have the money now."

"Wha—?" said Hambone. "Don't tell me it's reached the point now where girls are paying to have your clothes cleaned, Mitch."

"I knew he was popular with girls," said the saxophonist, "but I didn't know it went this far. Some people have all the luck."

Embarrassed, Douglas looked down at his drums. The tattoo became a little louder, a little faster. "Forget it, Rosemary," he said.

"Don't pay any attention to that moron," Hambone put in. "I'll let you take *my* raincoat to the cleaner's—and my shoes to the shoemaker's."

"I don't think you're one bit funny," Rosemary told him. "This is between me and Mi— Douglas."

"And I told you to forget it," said Douglas. His drumming became even louder, and the saxophonist punctuated the sound with a few notes on his horn.

But Hambone was still looking at her. "You know, Mitch, I wouldn't be so hasty. Rosemary's kind of cute."

"She's still in junior high," Douglas reminded him.

"Oh, that's right," said Hambone. "Isn't that too bad!" He winked at Rosemary before he turned back to the piano.

"Look, Rosemary," Douglas explained—overpatiently,

she thought. "We're rehearsing, so if you don't mind . . . I appreciate it about the coat and all, but don't worry about it. OK?"

"Yes. Sure," said Rosemary. She smiled awkwardly, gave him a sort of half wave, and hastily retreated. She felt humiliated again, even though she had tried to do the right thing. Douglas had a habit of humiliating her, she thought resentfully.

As she softly closed the door behind her, she could hear the boys picking up their music at the place where she had interrupted them. They were playing "I'm Getting Sentimental over You," with the saxophone coming on strong, but they didn't sound much like Tommy Dorsey's band, she decided with satisfaction.

She walked slowly down the street. Douglas thought she was peculiar. She knew he did. He didn't try to hide it. And because she had come to his house today, he probably also thought she was running after him. Apparently girls did. How terrible if he thought that of her, because it simply wasn't true. She loathed the sight of him.

Dear Daddy,

Are you *sure* you can't get home for Christmas? I mean, it has been *six months* since Mother and I saw you, and we both miss you very much. I know Seattle is a long way from here—and I know you are working in the band and traveling all over to make money for us, but I think I would rather be poorer and have a father.

The boy across the street has a band too. That is, he is trying to have one. He and his friends practice a lot, and we can't help hearing them. I think they have a long way to go, though.

Remember I told you that Franny, a girl who is on the paper with me, wrote an article about Thompson? It was supposed to be in the December issue of *The Green and the Gold,* but fortunately there isn't going to be room for it, so Franny says she will save it for a later issue. Maybe by that time she'll forget about it. I hope so. The less people know about Thompson, the better. . . .

Rosemary put her fountain pen down and chewed on a broken fingernail. She couldn't think of anything more to write about. Maybe it was because she didn't feel much like writing to her father at all. She was angry with him.

Her mother had looked angry too, when his letter came saying he would not be home for Christmas. Her face had gone all red as she read it, and she had said, "This is ridiculous!" in a tone that didn't sound at all amused, and then she had looked out the window, her chin stuck forward. For a moment her eyes had filled with tears, but she had fought them off very quickly. Since then she hadn't said anything about it, and Rosemary didn't know what she was thinking. Still, she thought she knew how her mother felt. They both understood her father's desire to earn some money for his family in the way he knew best, but the fact was, he wasn't sending back all that much. After all, hotel rooms were expensive.

The truth was that, in some secret part of her, Rosemary felt—and perhaps her mother did too—that her father really had abandoned them for a way of life that was more glamorous to him than anything Lynnfield had to offer. Rosemary couldn't blame him, in a way, because she had also heard the call of show business, but at the same time she couldn't *believe* he wouldn't be coming home to them at Christmas, of all times—that he wouldn't move heaven and earth to get there.

The year 1939 was winding down. Thanksgiving came and went. The Sunday after it was another dark rainy one. Rosemary's mother had gone off for the day with friends, so Malvina invited Rosemary to come along with her on the streetcar ride with Arthur. As a special treat, she said, the two of them could take in a movie when they reached the town at the end of the line. Their own town prohibited Sunday movies, so this was certainly a first for Rosemary. To see a movie on Sunday seemed deliciously wicked.

She had never had such a long streetcar ride before, and she enjoyed the novelty of it all. Beside her in a back seat, Malvina sat with her backbone stiff and straight and her expression formal, as if she felt constrained to be proper because she was Arthur's special guest. In spite of the rain, she was carefully dressed in a plain navy-blue coat and a plain navy-blue hat with a veil. She spoke very little, but with a kind of serious pride kept her eyes constantly on Arthur as he piloted the rocking streetcar along the wet tracks, made change and accepted fares, and told people to watch their step. They were traveling through the open countryside, but you could see little of it through the dirty steamed-up windows, and because the lights were on inside the car, dim though they were, the outside seemed darker in contrast. Occasionally they passed through small dreary mining communities. High slag heaps grew by the tracks, and the people who got on the car were drably dressed. Drops of rain dotted their cloth coats and jackets.

The weather had not improved by the time Rosemary and Malvina got off at the last stop, a coal town that had been hard hit by the Depression. In spite of somewhat better times, it still looked dirty and seedy in the rain and had an air about it of having given up the struggle.

Rosemary still felt expectant about the movie, however;

but it turned out to be a picture she had already seen, and not a good one at that. The sense of innocent sinfulness that had first affected her soon evaporated under feelings of restlessness, but she kept those feelings to herself, because Malvina, who had not seen the picture before, was enjoying it.

By the time the movie was over, the rain had changed to wet snow, but was still running in blackened rivulets down the sooty street, and Arthur had made the round trip back again and was going to treat them to a quick meal at a cafeteria. It had to be quick, because he had only half an hour for supper. Rosemary was extremely hungry by this time, but was afraid to eat much for fear Arthur couldn't afford it. She didn't suppose streetcar conductors made much money.

But Arthur said, "Now you have whatever you want, Rosemary. How about a nice ham sandwich?"

Unfortunately a ham sandwich cost twenty-five cents, and Rosemary couldn't help noticing that all Arthur had on his tray were a cup of coffee and a portion of rice pudding.

"Oh, I'm not very hungry," she said, her mouth watering at the sight of the ham. "Besides, my mother will have dinner ready when I get home. I might have some Jell-O now, though, if you don't mind."

"Why, sure," said Arthur. And as he reached over for the quivering red gelatin, Rosemary thought that he looked relieved.

Rosemary and Malvina got home at seven o'clock. By that time Rosemary was ravenous. She had been looking forward to finding a filling supper waiting for her, but all she found was Thompson sitting beside the refrigerator, indignant because she had not fed him since morning. Her mother was not there.

Wondering where she could be, Rosemary got out a can of cat food, but Thompson was so annoyed at his own hunger and at what he considered to be her slowness that he reached up and clawed at the tablecloth. The salt and pepper shakers and the sugar bowl crashed to the floor.

"Get out of here, you stupid cat!" Rosemary yelled at him.

Thompson tore dramatically out of the kitchen, skidding momentarily on the spilled sugar and scattering it around even more.

"What a mess," Rosemary groaned. She got the broom and the dustpan and was still in the process of sweeping it up when she heard Bingo barking downstairs and then her mother's footsteps coming up.

"I'm in here," she called.

Her mother stood in the doorway. "What on earth happened?"

"Thompson pulled the tablecloth down and everything on it. He was mad because I wasn't opening the can fast enough. I'm afraid he broke the sugar bowl."

"Oh, dear!" Her mother's voice sounded oddly trilly. Rosemary looked up curiously from her sweeping. Someone was standing behind her mother in the dimness of the hallway.

Her mother turned and took hold of the man's arm and drew him into the kitchen. "Paul, I want you to meet my daughter. Rosemary, this is Paul Scholz. We've just spent a wonderful afternoon in Pittsburgh with some friends of his."

Who was Paul Scholz that he should be introducing her mother to his friends? Unsmiling, Rosemary took the hand the stranger held out to her. He was a rather short, sturdily built man with thinning blond hair. Blue eyes smiled at her from behind his glasses. He certainly wasn't handsome. No threat. So why did she feel this sudden cold chill?

He held on to her hand, placing his other hand over it, and Rosemary's instant reaction was to try to pull away. He let her go, smiling as if he hadn't noticed.

Her mother took the broom and finished sweeping up the sugar and the broken bowl. "Paul's one of the partners down where I work," she was explaining. "I'm sure you've heard me speak of him." She was talking very fast. "We had a wonderful time this afternoon. . . . And how was your streetcar ride?"

"It was all right," Rosemary muttered. Not looking at either of them, she resumed opening the can of cat food.

"Paul and I have already eaten," said her mother. "Did you have something?"

"No!" said Rosemary.

"Well, fix yourself a sandwich or something," said her mother lightly. She and Paul went into the living room.

But Rosemary didn't feel like eating now, because there was a sinking feeling in the pit of her stomach. Dazedly she scooped some cat food out of the can and set it on the floor for Thompson, who had slunk back in and now began to eat as if he had been starved for days.

However, Rosemary had no desire to go into the living room with *them* either, so she got a book from her room and opened a can of kidney beans. She was sitting at the table, glumly eating out of the can and reading when Paul Scholz came back into the kitchen.

"Hi," he said tentatively. "Can I sit down?"

Somewhat surprised, Rosemary made a motion that was sort of a nod but was more like a shrug.

He sat opposite her. "You like kidney beans?" he said.

That was obvious, wasn't it? "Yes," she said.

"What are you reading? Oh, I see. Nancy Drew."

"I've outgrown Nancy Drew," Rosemary said coldly. "I just read them over again sometimes when I don't have anything else around to read."

"I see," said Paul Scholz.

What did he want from her? She wished he would go away.

"Your mother says you're quite a movie fan."

"Yes," said Rosemary.

"I like movies myself," he said. "I read *Gone With the Wind*, too. Now I'm anxious to see the picture."

He was trying to get on the good side of her. Why? Why should he? Rosemary's imagination leaped ahead. Was he thinking of marrying her mother? Was her mother so angry with her father that she was on the verge of divorcing him and marrying this man?

And then she, Rosemary, would have to live with them!

Sitting there so quietly, her fork poised over the can of kidney beans, Rosemary gave no hint to him of the sudden turmoil in her mind, but she couldn't make conversation.

She couldn't force herself to. Oh, go away, go away! she kept thinking, over and over.

And finally he did. He went back to the living room where her mother was waiting for him, and he said something to her, but he said it so low that Rosemary couldn't hear what it was. She couldn't hear her mother's answer either, but she did know that they were talking about her.

10

Rosemary scrunched down in her seat. Algebra class was in full swing, and she hoped the teacher, Mr. MacKay, would take no notice of her. He had been teaching them something new this morning, and the class had caught on quickly. Now Mr. MacKay stood at the blackboard writing down the steps in an equation as the class gave them to him, and there were so many hands in the air that he could not call on everyone who wanted to be called on. Something electric had taken place in class today; the students were enjoying themselves, actually being stimulated by the mathematical process, by the activity of their own minds, and by mutual rivalry. Mr. MacKay's face was flushed with excitement. Days like this did not happen very often, and he was obviously reveling in it.

Rosemary did not begrudge him his fun, but she felt completely out of things. For over a week she had been in a blue funk. Something had wedged itself between her and her mother, to whom she had always been so close, and that something was a man named Paul Scholz. Worse, it was a matter they could not discuss, and the stiffness between them seemed to increase every day.

Of course her mother had to see Paul at work, but she had been seeing him often outside the office, too, and last night he had come to dinner. He was behaving just like a suitor; in fact, they seemed to be having a whirlwind courtship. Rosemary wished her father knew; then he would surely come home. She wished there were some way to tell him that he was in danger of losing them both. But she couldn't be the one to do it—that was the trouble. It was sneaky to tattle.

And now, today, Rosemary hadn't been listening when Mr. MacKay explained the new material. She slunk down farther in her seat, her hands clasped tightly on her desk, and watched sourly as Ruth frantically waved her hand, was called on, and gave an answer, which Mr. MacKay wrote on the board with a flourish. Then Beany Segal rose to ask a question—an intelligent question. Mr. MacKay was answering him when the bell rang, announcing the end of class, and Rosemary gathered up her notebooks and textbooks with relief.

Ruth caught up with her as she went out the door. "Boy, that was fun!" she said. "I never enjoyed a class so much. I think math is my favorite subject."

"It's not mine," said Rosemary. She was glad they were now going to social studies class, where she would not feel so out of her depth. "Maybe the current-events papers will arrive today," she said, "and we can have a discussion about

Hitler and Stalin. That's what I like best—class discussions about real things."

"Oh, I like them too," Ruth conceded. She shifted her books into a more comfortable pile. "Say, have you heard the latest? Beany told me just before math class started. The town's going to flood the tennis courts!"

"They are?" Rosemary asked, amazed. "What for?"

"For ice skating, dummy! When it gets cold enough and the water freezes, we can ice skate."

"Oh-h!" said Rosemary, comprehending. Then she added, "But I don't have ice skates."

"That's all right," Ruth told her complacently, "neither do I. We'll ask for them for Christmas."

"Hm," said Rosemary, in doubt, "I hope it isn't too late. Christmas is only two weeks off."

"It can't hurt to ask," said Ruth.

That night after supper Rosemary's mother went out to a movie with Paul Scholz. "Be sure and go to bed early," she told Rosemary. "It's a school night."

"All right, but I have to go up to Ruth's for a minute," Rosemary said sullenly.

"Don't stay too long up there," her mother said, her voice brisk. Then, trailing the scent of perfume and ignoring Rosemary's long face, she went down the steps with Paul.

That made two nights in a row they were together, Rosemary thought, as she walked up to Ruth's. She was scared. Her mother seemed unapologetic, as if she felt she had a right . . .

Ruth had finished her homework when Rosemary arrived and was ready to explain the intricacies of the day's algebra lesson. Rosemary forced herself to listen, because she didn't want a repeat of her stupidity of that morning, and she soon caught on to what Ruth was talking about.

"I see," she said. "It's really simple, isn't it?"

"I can't understand why you thought it was hard in the first place," said Ruth.

"I can't either," said Rosemary in a voice of gloom.

"Is anything the matter?"

Rosemary shook her head. "No," she said. Actually, she longed to confide in somebody, and Ruth of all people would listen, but it seemed wrong to discuss her mother with an outsider. "I guess I was just daydreaming this morning in class," she said.

They were sitting in Ruth's bedroom. It was somewhat bigger than Rosemary's, with room for a desk and an old toy box full of stuffed animals and dolls that Ruth could not yet bear to part with. Several volumes of Bobbsey Twins books still reposed in the bookcase.

Rosemary glanced over at them. "Do you still read the Bobbsey Twins, for Pete's sake?" she asked.

"Of course not." Ruth grinned. She pulled one out and revealed a colorful magazine jacket hidden behind it. "I keep my *Weird Tales* back there," she said. "If I put them anywhere else my mother would find them and throw them out, but I'm supposed to keep the books dusted—and I do!"

"Very clever."

"Did you ask your mother about the ice skates?"

"Yes, but she said not to count on it."

"Well, we'll hope for the best." Suddenly Ruth's expression grew self-conscious. "Speaking of presents, I guess you know Sunday is my fourteenth birthday."

"Of course I know," said Rosemary. "Your birthday comes a week before Christmas, and mine comes two weeks after."

"My mother said I could invite you to dinner that night. Can you come?"

"Why, sure."

Ruth paused. "What are you going to bring me?"

"If I told you, it wouldn't be a surprise."

"I know, but—well, it would be such a waste of money if you bought me something I had, or didn't want."

"That's true," Rosemary conceded. "What would you like?"

Ruth thought for a minute, then said, "I could use a new movie star scrapbook. My last one is almost full. Or . . . a new *Weird Tales* should be out soon—but you'd have to hide that from my mother. You know what else I'd like: a manicure set. I don't know what they cost; maybe it would be too expensive."

"I'll see," said Rosemary. She rose to go, hesitated, then sat back down on the bed. Why should she leave early? she thought defiantly. Her mother wasn't home anyway.

"Fourteen," Ruth mused. "At least we won't be new teens any longer. People are always saying to me, especially my mother's friends, 'Oh, Ruthie, you're in your teens now, aren't you?' " She spoke in a high falsetto. Then she added, her eyes sparkling, "And in two years we'll be sixteen, and practically grown up. I'm looking forward to that."

Rosemary laughed. "But then they'll be saying, 'Oh, Ruthie, sweet sixteen and never been kissed'!"

"Yeck!" said Ruth. "I hate that phrase. It's so patronizing. Anyway"—she looked smug—"I *have* been kissed."

"You never!" said Rosemary.

"Yes, I have!"

"When? Why didn't you tell me?"

"I don't have to tell you everything, Rosemary Beedy."

"You're telling me now, though."

"Well, it was a long time ago."

"How long?"

"Halloween! The school dance."

Rosemary dismissed the idea with a wave of her hand. "Who would kiss you at the school dance, for heaven's sake?"

"Malcolm."

"Malcolm Gurney!"

"Certainly," said Ruth. "We were walking back toward the classroom, and we were passing Miss Alexander's room. It was all dark in there, and he suddenly grabbed me and pulled me inside the door and kissed me."

"Really?"

"Yes, really," said Ruth. "It was nice, I tell you."

"How was it nice?"

"It's hard to explain."

"Show me then."

"All right. Stand up." The girls got up, and Ruth took hold of Rosemary's shoulders. She pressed her lips against hers for a few seconds, then let her go. "Like that," she said.

"That's all?" said Rosemary, disappointed.

Ruth nodded.

"I don't think that's so much."

Ruth shrugged. "It's different when a boy kisses you," she said.

"I should hope so," said Rosemary, feeling a little jealous. She went over to the desk and gathered up her math book and notebook. "I guess I'd better leave before your mother kicks me out," she said with a sigh.

"I guess so," Ruth agreed. "I wish you didn't have to go home. I wish we had our own apartment. When we go to Hollywood, we will. Then we can talk all night if we want to."

"Yes," said Rosemary as they descended the stairs. "Let's promise each other." She stopped and held out her hand.

Ruth took the hand and shook it solemnly. "It's a promise," she said, and they continued down to the door, which she held open. "Gum-bye," she said. "See you tomorrow."

"Gum-bye," Rosemary said, and turned toward home.

The lights were on in the living room when she arrived at the Hauser house. As she stepped lightly onto the porch she could hear Malvina and the Hausers talking in there. They had the radio on, and Kate Smith was singing. Rosemary was about to go in when she heard Mrs. Hauser speak her mother's name. She stopped stock-still, her hand on the doorknob.

"It isn't that I don't sympathize with Anne," Mrs. Hauser was saying. "She must be very lonely with her husband away all this time. After all, he should be home looking after his family. But if she doesn't like being alone, she should get a divorce before she starts running around with other men. It doesn't look good."

"It's the child I feel sorry for," said Malvina. "Rosemary's so upset. Anyone can see that."

Mrs. Hauser tutted. "Poor little thing."

Out on the porch the "poor little thing" stood trapped, unable to enter. Tears began to fill her eyes. To feel herself pitied like this was a new experience.

"Someone should write to the father," said Mrs. Hauser, "tell him what's going on. . . ."

"Don't you dare do anything like that, Lottie," Mr. Hauser put in. "It's none of your business. I agree it's a bad situation, but you won't make it any better by butting in. You stay out of it. You hear?"

Rosemary stood riveted to the spot. She was not making a sound, but apparently Bingo had heard her breathing. He suddenly gave a little warning bark, came to the door, and barked again.

"What's the matter, Bingo?" Mr. Hauser called.

"Is someone out there?" Mrs. Hauser said sharply.

Rosemary scurried around to the side of the house. She heard Mrs. Hauser open the door. Bingo barked once more, and Rosemary flattened herself against the house. Mrs. Hauser must have had hold of Bingo's collar, because nothing happened, and soon she said, "False alarm, Bingo," and shut the door.

Rosemary let out a relieved gasp and felt her body relax. It felt so good, she thought, to have others agree with her that Paul Scholz did not belong in her mother's life, or hers, and at the thought she allowed a little tear of self-pity to run down her cheek.

But after a while, as she waited there in the darkness between the houses, another emotion began to take over. Those people had insinuated things about her mother that weren't nice, and she, Rosemary, hadn't rushed in to defend her. She had actually enjoyed it! She had felt sorry for herself instead.

Ashamed, she waited almost half an hour before again going back to the porch. The radio was silent now, and the Hausers and Malvina had all gone to bed. Rosemary let herself in and went upstairs. They'd never suspect she'd listened, but that didn't let her off the hook. She hadn't come to her mother's defense—it hadn't even occurred to her to—and how did you live with something like that?

11

The Dramatic Club, to which Rosemary belonged, had been rehearsing the Christmas play. Because there were few boys in the club, the play chosen consisted of early scenes from *Little Women*. Rosemary was playing Meg; Ruth was Amy. The director was the eighth-grade English teacher, a precise woman who gave elocution lessons after school. Rosemary had taken lessons from her for two years—before her father went away with the band and money became scarce—and during that time had acquired a small fame for giving "readings" at Sunday School and other functions. She had also learned to say "fy-er" instead of "far," when she meant *fire*, and to say "eye-ern," not "arn," for *iron*. But she had not missed Miss Draper or her lessons at all when they came to an end.

Rosemary had been studying her lines during the commercials of Lux Radio Theater. When the show ended, her mother asked, "Is Miss Draper directing the play?"

"Yes. She runs the Dramatic Club." Rosemary made a gagging sound.

"Rosemary! That isn't very nice."

"Well, if somebody else had it, there might be more boys. She's always correcting people's pronunciation."

"That's all to the good," said her mother. "Actors should speak well."

"I suppose so," said Rosemary. She was silent for a minute. "I guess you can't come to see the play. It'll be at assembly."

"Not if it's during the day. I have to work."

"If that Paul's so important in your office, you'd think he'd let you off."

"He's not my boss, Rosemary!"

"Hm." The radio show was over, so Rosemary gathered up her script, rose from the couch, and walked to the door. While she had her back turned, she said quickly, "Mother, are you going to divorce Daddy? Are you going to marry Paul?" Then she went cold all over.

To her horror, her mother didn't answer right away. After a few seconds, she said slowly, "I ... don't ... know."

Rosemary whirled around. "But don't you love Daddy anymore?"

"I don't . . . know that either. . . . Oh, I *do* love him, I guess, but he's been gone over six months, and he won't say when he's coming back. To all intents and purposes, he's deserted us."

"But he's *trying*. He's sending us money."

"A token," said her mother bitterly. "Only a token. What he's really supporting is his own vanity."

"How can you say that about Daddy?" Rosemary protested.

"I'm sorry," said her mother. She hesitated, then motioned toward the sofa. "Sit down again for a minute, Rosemary. I think we ought to talk. It's time we did. It's time we got all this out into the open."

Rosemary nodded without words. Flinging her script back on the coffee table, she did as her mother suggested. They sat at opposite ends of the couch facing each other; Rosemary tucked one leg underneath her.

Her mother gave her a weak smile. "Honey, I know you love your father. . . ."

"Yes, I do."

"And I know I shouldn't say bad things about him, but you asked me what was going on, and I want to explain. You've got to realize, Rosemary, that I'm still a young woman. I'm only thirty-three, and I have a life to lead, too. Maybe it's not as glamorous as your father's, but it's mine, and I want to lead it. Absence doesn't always make the heart grow fonder, you know. I hate to say it, but it's—it's getting hard for me even to remember what your father looks like. . . ."

Involuntarily Rosemary's glance went to her father's photograph, which was sitting on her mother's dressing table in a silver frame. Ordinarily, she never noticed it; it had become like part of the wallpaper. Now she looked at it intently, looked at the handsome black-haired young man with the funny haircut, the smooth unlined face, and the formal expression.

"Oh, that," said her mother, dismissing it. "That picture was taken over ten years ago. He's different now."

"Yes," said Rosemary bleakly, because she knew what

her mother meant. The young man in the photograph didn't really exist anymore. Her father had white in his hair now—a little—and his face was fuller. Like her mother, she couldn't quite picture him whole in her mind's eye as he was now. Was she forgetting too? she wondered in panic.

Her mother was watching her, waiting for her to say something more. Rosemary picked up her script again and hugged it against her chest. "I guess," she said finally, "this means you *are* going to marry Paul Scholz."

"I told you," said her mother, "I don't know. He's asked me to. Only I suppose I'm still testing my feelings. I just wish that . . ." Rosemary waited. "I wish you liked him a little. Can't you try? It would help. He's a very fine person, Rosemary."

"I don't care if he is," said Rosemary. "I hate him."

Without another word, she got up and went to her room, and when she reached it, she kicked the door hard, in frustration. But that didn't make her feel any better. Nothing could.

And then it was Christmas. At school *Little Women* was presented at assembly with hardly a hitch, and afterward each class had its own party in the homeroom. But that was only a prelude to what was usually the magic of Christmas Eve. As always, Rosemary and her mother were to have dinner at her grandparents' house on Christmas Day, but Christmas Eve had always been reserved just for them and Rosemary's father. It was then, ever since Rosemary had stopped believing in Santa Claus, that they had exchanged gifts and had their own close little celebration. This year, however, her father would not be home. Presents from him had arrived earlier, and he made a brief telephone call at suppertime, saying he was lonely and would be with them in spirit. But that was not the same thing. For one thing, neither Rosemary nor her mother could think of anything to say to him—after all, too much lay between them—and later Rosemary felt cheated. She wished she had somehow been more at ease.

After the call she and her mother were getting ready to go to church when Rosemary heard footsteps on the stairs. She looked down them in surprise to see Paul Scholz approaching her. "Merry Christmas," he said.

He had brought *her* a present. Rosemary didn't even want to open it. He sat there in the living room, a glass of wine in his hand, a pleasant smile on his face, as if he liked her very much, and all she could think about was how much she hated him and resented his being there. After all, why should he give her a present? He'd only known her a little over a month.

"Open it, Rosemary," said her mother. Sitting close to Paul, she gave him a conspiratory sidelong glance, as if they had some delightful secret between them, as if this bribery were going to make everything all right.

Rosemary sat down on a stool opposite them. Obediently she removed the red ribbon from around the package, then ran her finger beneath the folds of the wrapping paper and laid it back. The box was a fairly large one. She took the cover off and pulled aside the tissue paper in the box. Figure skates, white figure skates . . .

She had wanted ice skates, surely. She had tried not to nag, but she had *really* wanted them. If she could have had only one present this Christmas, the skates would have been her choice. But not from him. Never from him. She sat staring down at the box, not knowing how to behave.

"Aren't you going to say thank you, Rosemary?"

"Thank you."

"I hope they fit," said Paul. "Why don't you try them on?"

"All right," said Rosemary. She felt she ought to be polite as she slipped off her shoes and pulled on the skates and laboriously tied them. As she stood up on wobbly feet, Paul came over and steadied her. "They fit fine," said Rosemary.

"Now you can learn to skate like Sonia Henie," said Paul.

"Yes," she replied in a dull voice. But she didn't intend to use them at all. Oh, why couldn't her *mother* have given her the skates?

"They make your legs look so nice," said her mother approvingly. "But," she added, "I think you'd better take them off now. They won't do the carpet much good."

Paul laughed and helped Rosemary back to her stool.

Later, after church, Ruth breathlessly rushed up to Rosemary and her mother. "I'm getting the skates for Christmas," she burbled. "Are you?"

"Yes," said Rosemary.

"Now all we need is some ice. I wish it'd get colder."

But Rosemary didn't. She hoped there'd never be any ice.

12

One evening a few days after Christmas, just as Rosemary and her mother were coming indoors, Mrs. Hauser emerged from her domain and stopped them in the hallway. Her face was solemn and full of pity; yet it masked a kind of secret enjoyment as she droned, "Rosemary, you're just the person I want to see. Poor child! Your holidays have been so bleak, haven't they? With your father not here and all . . ."

"Oh, I don't know," said Rosemary, mentally backing away.

"Well, anyway," Mrs. Hauser continued, "Earle and I have talked it over and decided we'd like to have a little get-together tomorrow night—not for the grown-ups, but just for the young people, and for you especially, Rosemary. Won't that be nice? And we want you to invite anybody you like—say, a couple of other girls. That would be fine. And my nephew Douglas knows about it. I've told him to come. He'll probably bring a friend or two, too."

"Oh, no!" Rosemary wailed. Mrs. Hauser was doing it

again, pushing her on Douglas and believing she was doing her a favor. How *could* she? Douglas was going to hate this.

"Why, Rosemary!" said her mother. "How ungrateful you sound! I think that's lovely, Mrs. Hauser. Of course Rosemary's delighted."

"Oh, I'm sure she'll enjoy it," said Mrs. Hauser. Her face brimmed with self-satisfaction. "And remember, you don't have to do a thing, Rosemary—just come down. I'll make some popcorn and lemonade and maybe buy some little candies. Now don't forget. It's tomorrow night. Be sure and tell your little friends."

Rosemary smiled sickly and managed to breathe a weak "OK," but once she was upstairs in the privacy of their room, she beat her fists against the pillows of the couch in a state of impotent fury.

"I wish I were dead!" she cried. "Oh, Mother, do I have to go?"

"I'm afraid you do," she said. "After all, as I've said many times, Mrs. Hauser means well."

"I just wish she didn't, that's all! I just wish she didn't."

Her mother laughed. "I don't think you'd want her as an enemy, either."

And Rosemary, remembering Mrs. Hauser's remarks about her mother, was suddenly still. Then she said, "Douglas is going to think I'm chasing him. And I'm not! I'm not! I don't even like him very much."

"Maybe Douglas understands. She's his aunt, you know. Besides, it may not be as bad as you think."

"No," said Rosemary, "it'll be worse. Oh, Mother, how do you think she managed to talk him into it?"

"I have no idea," said her mother. "It's just likely she didn't have to. Perhaps he wants to come."

But Rosemary knew he didn't. She knew Mrs. Hauser was having this party out of pity for her, because she thought Rosemary's parents were acting selfishly. She had prevailed upon Douglas to come by using that same argument. He would be here, all right, because he felt it was his duty, because he felt sorry for her.

Rosemary writhed with shame.

Thinking about it more calmly the next day, however, she decided that if she had to go through with the party, she at least ought to look as pretty as possible. Then no one could say she hadn't tried. What was more important, she intended to *behave* as normally as possible, too, not peculiarly. The party was a fact; she could not get out of it; and this was one time she was determined that nothing go wrong.

That night she put on her new plaid dress with the gored skirt that her mother had given her for Christmas and topped it off with the casual white sweater her father had sent her. Clad also in pristine new saddle shoes and with a beanie, like the one Bette Davis had worn after her brain operation in *Dark Victory*, bobby-pinned to her hair, she was nervous but presentable. She was just about to descend the stairs when the sound of a trombone playing "Blue Skies" hit her ears. The melody was then picked up by a dance band.

"Someone must have brought a phonograph," said her mother.

"That's Benny Goodman's band," said Rosemary, who prided herself on recognizing the individual bands.

"Well, aren't you going down?"

"Yes," said Rosemary. But she couldn't just yet. Her heart was in her mouth. She knew to whom the phonograph and the records belonged; the sound of them had often drifted to her from across the street.

She took a gulp of air. "All right," she said finally, and she forced herself to go down, step by slow step.

She just had time to see Douglas and his pal Hambone bent over a phonograph in a corner of the living room when the doorbell jangled. Relieved, Rosemary turned to answer it, and found Ruth and Ginger Oppenheimer on the porch. At least now she would not have to face the boys alone. As she helped her friends remove their coats, Rosemary thought they looked beautiful, if a little awed at the sight of the high school boys in the living room. In fact, she didn't think the boys had any reason to complain about spending the evening with three junior high school girls. At least not these three particular junior high school girls.

"Too bad there isn't one more boy," Ruth whispered.

Rosemary ignored her. They entered the living room, and the boys sort of stood at attention.

"Well!" said Douglas, with a heavy attempt at lightness. "There certainly are enough girls to dance with."

"You bet," said Hambone. "Pretty ones, too." He winked at Rosemary.

"If we're going to dance," Douglas said, "we ought to get this rug rolled back."

"I'll help you," said Hambone.

Glad to have something to do, the boys bent down and rolled the rug into a cylinder. They carried it to the hall and dropped it there.

"Now," said Douglas, coming back and brushing off his hands, "who's going to dance with me? Rosemary? Hambone, put another record on."

As Hambone flipped over the record that was already on the turntable, Rosemary backed away from Douglas slightly. She was afraid to dance with him; she would make a fool of herself; she would step all over his feet.

"I think you boys ought to dance with my guests first," she said, seizing a chance to postpone the inevitable, "since there are more of us than there are of you."

"That's OK with me," said Hambone. He turned to Ginger and swept her into the middle of the floor. "What's your name?"

"Oh, I'm sorry; I didn't introduce you," Rosemary cried. "Ginger, this is Hambone. His real name is Kenneth. Hambone, this is Ginger."

Hambone and Ginger were already dancing happily with each other. Hambone looked at Rosemary over Ginger's shoulder and winked at her again. But she had made her first mistake.

Douglas was already dancing with Ruth, who was a good dancer, Rosemary knew. Her brother had taught her, and she had taught Rosemary. Douglas seemed to enjoy dancing with her.

Rosemary edged over toward the phonograph. She felt awkward standing there by herself, so she leaned over the pile of records Douglas and Hambone had brought with them and looked through them. All the good bands were here: Goodman, the Dorseys, Glenn Miller, and Artie Shaw, plus some Rosemary wasn't familiar with, such as Red Nichols and Harry James. If I ever get rich, she thought, I'm going to have a phonograph and buy all these records for myself.

The record on the phonograph came to an end. "Want me to play another?" she asked. "Is it all right if I pick one out?"

"I'll do it," said Douglas. He took a record off the pile and put it on the turntable. Then, before the music had time to start, he turned to her and said, "OK, Rosemary. It's your turn."

He took her into his arms and the music began. It was another Goodman, "And the Angels Sing." Rosemary felt stiff as a board; she was afraid her feet weren't going to move. What would he think if he knew she had never danced with a boy before?

Douglas gave her a little shake. "Relax," he said. And the next thing she was actually dancing with him.

He turned out to be a firm, easy-to-follow leader, but in her nervousness she missed the first few steps. "Sorry," she murmured.

He looked down at her, and she noticed that her eyes came about level with his chin. Although his skin looked as if a hair had never appeared there, he smelled of shaving lotion. The smell made her feel dizzy. "That's all right," he said. "There's nothing to be nervous about."

She remembered then that Ruth had told her you should

never apologize to a boy if you missed a step. You should both pretend it was his fault, even if both of you knew it wasn't. In fact, *he* should apologize to *you*.

Her second mistake.

Still, she wasn't doing too badly. She danced with Hambone next, and it was even easier than with Douglas. Funny, but she felt more comfortable in every way with Hambone. Even when he tried to steer her under the mistletoe that Mrs. Hauser had coyly hung in the doorway, she was able to laugh and say, "No, Hambone, I don't want to kiss you."

The boys danced with each girl in turn, and then, for good measure, clowned by dancing with each other. The girls took turns changing the records. Rosemary was proud of her friends. They were killing themselves to appear grown up in the eyes of these high school boys, and they hardly giggled at all. She was glad, too, that she had learned how to do the shag and the Suzy Q and all the other popular steps, not to mention the fox trot. If she made a few wrong steps, they weren't too glaringly wrong, she thought.

Oh, her mother had been right. The party wasn't so bad at all. Why, she was having fun! And she was sure the boys were too. She would have to thank Mrs. Hauser, tell her how grateful she was for this wonderful, unforgettable evening. Oh, yes, thank you, dear Mrs. Hauser, thank you.

The smell of popcorn had been wafting in from the kitchen for some time. Soon Mrs. Hauser appeared and said, "Why don't you all stop dancing for a while and have some refreshments?" And then she and Malvina and Rosemary's mother brought in the popcorn and candy and homemade cookies, and Cokes, too.

Douglas turned the phonograph down low as the boys and girls helped themselves to food. Then they sat around eating for a while. There was a little desultory conversation, like "Um. Good cookies!" or "Would you like a Coke?" but unfortunately, with the cessation of activity, the limitations of the evening had now become apparent. The girls and boys could find nothing in common with each other. Along with the difference in age, they went to different schools. They had nothing, really, to say to one another.

"Hey!" said Rosemary a little desperately. "Does anybody know any games?"

"Yes," said Hambone, who was sitting on the arm of her chair, "post office."

"Can't you think about anything except kissing?" Douglas asked him.

"No," said Hambone. "Can you?"

"I know a game," said Ginger. "My cousin taught it to me. It's called Psychology."

"Oh? How do you play that?" asked Douglas, leaning against the door frame. He looked bored, Rosemary thought. It had been better when they were dancing.

"It's not hard," said Ginger. "Somebody says a word, and then the next person says the first thing that comes into his mind, no matter what it is. For instance, I might say 'bread,' and then you'd say 'butter.' "

"Sounds kind of dumb," said Hambone. "How do you make points?"

"You don't, I guess. It's just for fun. Sometimes it can be very funny."

"We might as well try it," said Douglas. He sat down, legs tucked under him tailor fashion, on the floor next to the couch and took a sip of Coke. "All right," he said, turning to Ginger, "the word is *podiatrist.*" His face was serious.

Ginger looked blank. "I'm afraid I don't know what that is," she said.

"That's all right," said Douglas. "You just said what came into your head."

Ginger looked at Ruth. "Miss Draper," she said.

"Old fusspot," said Ruth, and laughed. She turned to Rosemary. "William Holden."

Rosemary caught herself about to say, "Douglas," but stopped herself in time. "Movie star," she answered blandly, and she looked up at Hambone. "Apple pie," she said.

"Ice cream," said Hambone, and the game went around the circle again, somewhat predictably and dully.

But Ruth was not unmindful of what usually went on in Rosemary's head. She was, after all, her best friend and confidante. Therefore, when her turn came around again, she smiled at Rosemary and said quickly, "Mitch Mitchell."

"Cap pistol," said Rosemary, and immediately froze.

Silence flowed in. Then, "What does that mean?" asked Ginger.

"Hey, wait a minute," said Hambone. "I think I know! Mitch, do you remember that day one summer before you moved away when Rosemary came up and got into a fight with you? She instigated it. What a little brat!" He laughed. "And you really whaled her. Say, Rosemary, I'll bet you never did get your cap pistol back."

"No," said Rosemary, "I didn't. And I think this is a stupid game." She turned to Ruth furiously. She was so angry that she couldn't wait till they were alone to say what she thought. "That was a mean cowardly thing to do," she said.

"Cowardly! How do you get cowardly out of that? You're the one who's cowardly. It's only a game, for heaven's sake!"

Rosemary glanced over at Douglas, who looked embarrassed. Was he always to feel embarrassed in her presence? she wondered. She looked away hurriedly and glared again at Ruth, who had assumed an air of hurt innocence.

Hambone, for one, had perked up. The game was turning out to be lively, after all. "I don't think," he said, as though he were discussing a scientific problem, "that you can call Rosemary cowardly either, Ruth. I've seen her do some pretty spunky things. You weren't there that day in the garage, but she was a real hellion, let me tell you. And she was littler than Mitch, too."

Oh, *please* stop talking about it, Rosemary thought in agony.

"You're wrong," said Ruth. "Rosemary's scared of a lot of things."

"Name one," Rosemary put in boldly. If they insisted on talking about her, she might as well defend herself.

"We-l-l," said Ruth, pondering the question. "Boys, for one thing, but I guess that's natural. You're also scared of"—her eyes flashed—"the Wakely house!"

"Oh, I am not."

"You are too. How about that day we snuck in? You wouldn't stay in there a minute even. You ran right out again." She turned to the others. "Rosemary thinks the Wakely house is haunted."

The others laughed. "Do you really, Rosemary?"

"I do not!"

"In that case," said Ruth, her eyes dancing with mischief, "I guess you wouldn't be afraid to prove it. I mean, you wouldn't be scared to go there at night. Like now, for instance."

"Why . . . no. . . ." Ruth had to be kidding.

"By yourself," Ruth added. "All alone."

Rosemary paused. Ruth wasn't kidding. She glanced around at the others. They were all waiting for her answer, and she was about to make her third mistake.

"I dare you," said Ruth.

The party is over, Rosemary thought.

Rosemary couldn't *believe* this was happening to her. One moment she was at a party, having a perfectly marvelous time—or she had been when they were dancing—and now they were all out on the street, and she was carrying Mr. Hauser's flashlight. Mrs. Hauser had protested at the turn the get-together had taken, but they had told her they had to go out to settle a dare. They didn't tell her that all of them but Rosemary were going to wait at the corner while she broke into the Wakely house, went up to the tower room on top, and waved the flashlight around to prove she was there.

The night was dark, but on the way up the hill, Christmas lights from houses along the way pierced the gloom with a bright sense of warmth and welcome. Up by the Wakely house, however, the streetlight on the corner was the only light anywhere, and it somehow made everything seem darker.

"This is kind of silly," said Douglas. "Are you sure you want to go through with it?" he asked Rosemary.

"I certainly do," she told him, but she did not feel as confident as she sounded. They had reached the house now, and her knees seemed to be buckling.

"It looks awfully dark and scary," said Ruth, who was peering through the gate. "I wouldn't want to go in there now, even if all of you went along. Come on, Rosemary, I'm sorry. It was just a joke. You don't have to go through with it. Let's go back and dance some more."

Rosemary almost weakened. From under her eyelashes she stole a look at Douglas. It was hard to read what he was thinking as he stared silently at the Wakely house. Would he think she was weak if she backed down? She did not know why she cared so much, but she wanted to make a good impression on him.

But Hambone had said she was spunky. That was a nice thing to be, and she wanted Douglas to admire—

"No," she said, "I accepted the dare and we've come all this way. I'll do it."

"OK," said Ruth, as if washing her hands of all responsibility for what might happen, "somebody help her over the fence. We'll wait at the corner, Rosemary. We can see the tower better from there."

The next thing Rosemary knew, Hambone had lifted her up so that she could grasp the top of the wall and pull herself over. Fleetingly she thought of her new dress and hoped she wouldn't tear it, although that didn't seem like the most important thing at the moment.

She dropped to the ground on the other side. "So long," she called. She stood there for a second, then took a deep breath, switched on the flashlight, and forced herself to walk toward the house. All she could do now was get it over with fast, so that she could return to the comfort of her friends.

The night might have seemed brighter if there were snow on the ground, she thought, or if there were stars. As it was, though, she could see the bare branches of the trees against the whiteness of the house. Kicking through the fallen leaves in her path, Rosemary watched its huge bulk fill her view. She flashed her light over the white stucco, and from a window a reflection of the beam glinted back at her. Fear and dread had her in an icy grip now. The house looked empty and hollow, but somehow so expect-ant. . . . She stopped, unable to go any farther, tempted to turn and run back the way she had come. Her breath was coming out in short gasps.

But if she went back they'd laugh at her. Maybe not right away, while they, too, felt the house's dark spell, but later perhaps. She knew they would.

She made herself go on. Picking her way now in the glow of the flashlight, she went around to the side door where, she remembered, she and Ruth had entered the house before.

The door was still open. No one had been there since.

She tried to keep her mind a blank as she entered the house and was enveloped by the total darkness. On one side, she knew, the cellar yawned as if waiting to bury her alive, so she hurried up the little staircase and went into the hallway, leaving doors open behind her in case she had to run out again quickly. A breeze blew through the door, rustling things in the kitchen. Something white drifted into the air from the floor, seemed to stand there for a second, then fell back down. Rosemary stifled a shriek and flashed the light on it. Only an old newspaper. There was no furniture in the room, just newspapers scattered everywhere.

Another door led into the main hallway, and her light showed her the white staircase winding up into the darkness. She was shaking now as she crept forward, and her teeth were chattering. Behind her the newspapers rustled, like long dresses sweeping the floor. She flashed the light upward. High over the staircase as it wound from floor to floor she could just make out the outlines of the tower. That was where she had to go . . . *had* to go. But instead, she stood there, again unable to move. Fear was suffocating her. She wanted to get out of here! And yet, if she turned and ran . . . something . . . might follow her.

Slowly she moved one foot forward, then the other. As

she advanced she could feel the house closing in on her. It seemed to be aware of her presence, as if it had a mind of its own.

Outside the breeze picked up. She was aware of it fingering at the eaves, finding holes into which to whisper. She thought she heard a cry somewhere in the midst of it.

There was only one thing to do. Mindlessly, she ran up the steps, around and around. Somehow she reached the tower, and when she did, she flashed her light wildly at the little windows, and the reflection flashed back at her, white, blinding. She had spots before her eyes as she turned and stumbled back down again.

The stairs! This was where Aurora Wakely had also come down, groping her bloody way, vainly seeking help. And she, Rosemary, would have to pass that spot once more if she was to escape.

No, she thought, there was no Aurora Wakely. Ruth had made it up.

Hadn't she? She *had* said she had.

With her back against the wall, Rosemary slumped into a sitting position on the step. What if her friends had tired of waiting and gone home? Then she would be truly alone here.

She could hear a pulse thumping in her ears. She didn't believe in ghosts, she kept telling herself. And yet . . . and yet it could be that some houses, some places, had a mood. Perhaps they retained within their boards the memory of strong feelings experienced there. This house seemed to have absorbed such an atmosphere. In the cold darkness it had such a mood. And having the flashlight with her made it worse in a way. Its light seemed to be fading, growing dim, and she had the sense that at any minute its little yellow beam would illuminate a figure on the stairs below her, an unnamed intelligence that still felt it belonged here, even though it might have forgotten the emotions that had set it loose in the first place.

Any minute she expected—in fact, she did think she heard—what sounded like the echo of a scream bouncing off the walls, bouncing off itself, yet insubstantial and not existing anywhere except in the mind, like something unheard, as a tree falling in a lonely forest is unheard by human ears.

Any second now Rosemary expected to experience that unheard scream and, pushing her back against the wall, she braced herself for it, her skin cold, her hair prickling on her head. She was afraid to breathe.

And there *was* a voice, even though the wind had arisen outside and was distorting the sound. "Ro-ose-ma-ry!" it called. "Ro-ose-ma-ry!"

In the hall below, a windblown sheet of newspaper scudded along the floor as Rosemary, shaking and sobbing, her back still to the wall, slid slowly to her feet. "I'm up here," she called in a faint voice, and then, more loudly, "Douglas, I'm up here."

He was holding on to the wall and feeling his way in the dark. She lifted her hand and shone the light on the floor. He came closer. "Come on down. Let's go home now."

But Rosemary just stood there. She couldn't move; she felt cold all over. Douglas came up the steps two at a time. He took her hand and pulled her toward him. He took her trembling body into his arms and held her close to him. And, oh, suddenly she felt warm and safe.

"What happened?" he asked, a note of alarm in his voice.

"N-n-nothing!"

"Then why are you shaking so?"

"I-I'm s-s-scared."

"What a dumb thing," he said, "coming in here in the middle of the night. Someone might have been in here. A tramp or something. That's why I followed you, but I couldn't see where I was going and you got ahead of me."

Gently he led her down the steps. It was his infinite gentleness that got to her and made the tears roll faster down her cheeks. She had never dreamed that he was the kind of person who could be like this. She had always thought he was aloof and maybe even a little mean. But he was wonderful—*wonderful!*—in every way.

He removed the flashlight from her limp, unresisting hand and flashed what was left of its beam ahead of them.

"Wh-where are the others?" Rosemary whispered. "I hope they saw the light in the t-tower. I'd hate to think I did it all for . . . n-nothing."

"They must have seen it," he said. "They said they were going to wait at the corner." He paused and glanced back at the dark, silent, waiting stairway. "Did you really go all the way up?"

"Yes, I really did," she said. She was still holding on to his hand for dear life, drawing bravery from its warmth.

She heard Douglas make a breathy sound, as if he were laughing a little. "Boy!" he said. "You don't have much sense, but I have to admit it, as Hambone says, you sure do have spunk."

"Th-thanks," said Rosemary, and she walked closer to him as they escaped from the house and walked down the drive toward the iron gate. She was beginning to be able to breathe naturally again. Her trembling had died down too, and the tears on her face were drying. She wasn't afraid anymore. Instead, she was aware now of a different emotion, one about which she had no doubt.

Oh, Douglas! she thought. I love you, I love you, I love you!

13

Rosemary Beedy, high school girl, sat in a beautiful park in the moonlight. Douglas Mitchell, now a senior, and star of both the football and basketball teams, emerged from out of the darkness and sat by her side.

"Hello, Rosemary," he said softly.

"Oh, Douglas . . ." She smiled up at him and saw, mirrored in his eyes, the same love she felt in her own heart and had kept hidden until only this moment.

"Rosemary, I've been thinking about us."

"Yes, Douglas?"

"I'd be honored—and so happy—if you'd wear my new school ring. I want you to be my girl, Rosemary—go steady with me. Will you?"

"Oh, yes, Douglas!"

"Darling! I was so afraid I'd lose you to someone else. . . ."

Rosemary Beedy, junior high school girl, who, at least, was now fourteen, sighed with longing and gazed out the schoolroom window at the falling snow. It was no good, she thought, this daydreaming, because daydreams never came true. At any rate, she had never had any that did. No. She would have to curb herself of the habit. After all, if you wanted something to happen, you were wiser not to think about it at all. Then, if it happened, it would be all the sweeter. She had had many daydreams in the two weeks since the Wakely house adventure, but nothing had changed. Douglas went about his business as usual, nodding his head politely when he saw her, but otherwise paying no attention to her. *She* might remember the moment he put his arms around her and held her safe, but he apparently didn't.

Oh, daydreams were so satisfying, she thought wistfully, but she simply had to stop the habit.

But if Douglas hadn't changed, other things had after the first of the year. She couldn't be sure, but she thought the change had begun the Saturday afternoon she returned from the movies and found her mother on the telephone. It was easy to remember which Saturday it was. On their way home she and Ruth had, as usual, stopped to look for ice on the tennis courts. Rosemary would have liked to put aside her skates, considering how she got them, but Ruth, in her enthusiasm, would not let her. In spite of herself, Rosemary became infected by the fever to skate, but day after day they stood beside the courts, their heads hanging in disappointment.

The day before this one, however, they had found a slushy mess, something like melting sherbet, covering the courts. It had not been anywhere near adequate enough to skate on then, but today there was real ice, hard, skate-upon-able ice. In fact, a few people had already discovered it and were skating!

The girls rushed home, and Rosemary ran up the steps two at a time, slamming the stair door behind her. "Mother!" she yelled. "There's ice! There's real honest-to-goodness ice!" She burst into the living room. "Can I go skating after supper with Ruth? There are going to be lots of people there. They're going to have lights and everything!"

Her mother was talking on the telephone, talking earnestly. While she talked, she ran her hand through her hair in an unconscious nervous manner. As Rosemary barged in, she put the hand over the mouthpiece. "Rosemary, can't you see I'm on the phone?" Her eyes were troubled.

"But—" said Rosemary.

Her mother spoke into the phone. "I'll be right back," she said. She put the receiver down and walked over to the door and gently pushed Rosemary out of the room. Then she quietly but firmly closed the door.

Amazed, Rosemary stood there for a minute. Her mother had never done anything like that before. They had never had secrets.

She was dying to know what was going on, but realized that if she stayed here, her mother would think she was listening, so she went back to her room. Thompson was curled up on the bed. She sat beside him and stroked him idly. She didn't know why, but she had the distinct impression that her mother had been talking to her father. Maybe it was something she had happened to hear her mother say when she first walked in: "It's up to you," she had said.

Thinking back later, Rosemary was sure that things had changed after that day. She was sure that that was when Paul Scholz stopped coming to the house. Certainly, by the end of January, she realized that she had not seen him for a long time.

Dear Daddy,

Everybody thought it never would, but the water in the tennis courts finally froze last week for two days, and Ruth and I got to use our skates. I was sure I was going to be very good at it. I had imagined myself swirling around like Sonia Henie, maybe even running on the tips of my skates—you know the way she does—why, the only thing missing would be Tyrone Power to fall in love with me. But guess what, I could hardly stand up. My ankles felt weak as anything.

Even so, I'm happy to be able to tell you I didn't fall down. Ruth did, twice.

Rosemary broke off, biting the end of her pen. She wasn't going to tell her father what else had happened, or, rather, hadn't happened. Douglas had been there, but he hadn't asked her to skate with him. She had thought he would, when she saw him there. She had expected it after what had occurred in the Wakely house. But all he had done was smile at her once.

Her father didn't know about Douglas—that is, he didn't know how she felt about him—and so she didn't have to tell him how Douglas and Hambone had clowned around on their skates in front of a girl on the sidelines who didn't have any. Rosemary had no idea who the girl was and had no desire to know.

Remembering it all now, she sighed, then returned to her letter.

A horrible thing happened yesterday. *The Green and the Gold* came out and Franny's article was in it, the one she wrote last fall about me and Thompson and had to postpone. Remember, I told you about it. She called it "The Rich Cat," and told how Thompson had inherited all that money, or would if we didn't treat him right. I don't think she meant it to be mean or anything, but it came out that way. I have never felt so *humiliated*! But even that wasn't the worst thing. The paper was delivered to the kids at the end of the school day yesterday, so nobody had time to read it until they got home. This morning, when I got to school, a whole bunch of boys was lined up around the flagpole, and Ruth and I had to walk past them, and when we did they started meowing and calling out, "Here, kitty, kitty, kitty!" They kept it up all the time we were walking into the building, until we were inside. People kept teasing me that way all day long, and even two of the teachers asked me how my cat was. Franny apologized, but of course by then it was too late. Mother says they'll all forget about it soon, but I wonder.

Not everything is bad, though. Tomorrow they are having tryouts for the operetta. This year it's about Switzerland, with three leading girls and three leading boys and some smaller parts. Both Ruth and I are going to try out. Oh, I hope I can be in it.

The operetta, which was presented every March, was the biggest event of the school year. Everyone was involved. The orchestra took part; singers from the seventh, eighth, and ninth grades made up the chorus; other students were in group dances. The leading parts, however, were always taken by ninth graders, and Rosemary thought she would die if she didn't get one. After all, she wanted to be an actress, didn't she? And if she couldn't get a part in a school operetta and get started on her way, how could she ever get to Hollywood?

The tryouts were held after school, in the auditorium. The hopefuls had been asked to bring something to sing, and Miss Alexander, the music teacher, who would be in charge of the music in the operetta, was there to accompany them. She would also help pick the cast, along with Miss Draper, director of the acting, and the gym teacher, who would take care of the dances.

Rosemary had never really sung before an audience before. As Miss Draper's elocution student, she had done readings, and she had acted in the Christmas play, of course, and she had once been a contestant in a quiz show in assembly, but singing was different. Oh, she sang a lot around the house; in fact, Mrs. Hauser said she just loved to hear her. One time she had told Rosemary she sounded just like Deanna Durbin or Jeanette MacDonald. That had given Rosemary confidence, and she had sung all the louder every time she washed the dishes.

Here in the auditorium that confidence was all draining away. The place was full of people. There were the boys Miss Alexander had roped into trying out, using wiles only she knew about, who were lounging in the seats looking bored; there were lots of girls, twice or three times as many girls as boys, each one of them thinking she was right for the leading role; and then, of course, there were the teachers involved, and the principal, who had slipped in quietly and was sitting in a back seat smiling and looking interested. Even the janitor was using the excuse of sweeping the hall floor by the middle door, so he could watch what was going on.

Rosemary had been getting more and more tense all afternoon; now her hands were sweaty and she was finding it hard to breathe naturally. She had decided to sing "Over the Rainbow," because she knew it so well she could sing it without thinking and was thus less likely to make a mistake. Still, when they called her name, she gave a start, and Ruth had to push her to her feet. Feeling like a zombie, she went up the little stairway to the stage and stood there looking down at the floor, trying not to see the people in front of her. Dimly, she heard Miss Alexander playing the lead-in to her song. Rosemary cleared her throat. Miss Alexander played it again.

"Meow!" said a voice from the audience.

Miss Alexander stood up. "Now, Arnold, you stop that, or I'll make you leave."

"Oh, I'll be glad to leave, Miss Alexander. . . ."

"Never mind," she said. "I'll give you the leading part. How would you like that?"

"You wouldn't like it either," he told her. Rosemary heard some giggles and wished she were a million miles away.

"All right, Rosemary, we'll try it again," said the teacher. "Don't be frightened, child."

Rosemary smiled bleakly.

Miss Alexander played the introduction again, and Rosemary now realized with horror that she was playing the verse, which Rosemary didn't know so well, instead of the chorus. She tried to remember the words . . . "When all the world is a hopeless jumble" . . . something like that. Her voice seemed to be coming from down inside a barrel somewhere, way off in the distance. It didn't even sound like her voice.

She closed her eyes. This would be over soon, she told herself, and at that thought she got out a few notes that had breath behind them. Then, as if startled at what she had done, she quavered and stopped. Miss Alexander nodded encouragement and started the introduction all over again. Rosemary gave her another sick smile and began the verse from the beginning once more. She raced through it, mumbling the words she wasn't sure of, her voice weak and wavery. All she wanted was for the agony to be over with, and as she reached the chorus, she noticed that Miss Alexander was playing faster and faster to keep up with her.

But then Miss Alexander did a surprising thing; she sang the chorus right along with Rosemary. At the sound of another voice blending with hers, Rosemary regained some confidence, and only by the time she reached the end of the song did she become aware that she was again singing alone, but singing much better, almost as well as she did in her private concerts in the kitchen, her voice filling the hall.

She hardly heard the slight scattering of applause that followed her back to her seat, she was so relieved that it was over. But even as calm descended upon her, Rosemary knew she had not done her best. Oh, why couldn't she have been brave from the beginning? She would never get to Hollywood at this rate. And people would never know how dazzling she really could be.

"You were very good," Ruth said in a bland voice.

"No, I wasn't. I was terrible! Don't lie to me."

"Well . . ." said Ruth. "You got better there toward the end."

"I was scared."

"I'm not," said Ruth. "I don't care whether I get a part or not."

"Why are you here then?" Rosemary asked.

"Well, if you get a part, I want to be in it too, even though I'm not much for singing. We always do things together, don't we?"

That surprised Rosemary, because Ruth usually took the lead in the things they did, but she didn't have time to answer. Miss Alexander had called Ruth to the stage. Because she didn't care, Ruth walked up confidently. "I'm going to sing 'The Three Little Fishes,' " she said, and then she proceeded to do so, cockily, brashly, and delightfully. When she had finished she gave a little bow to the round of sincere applause that greeted her, and Rosemary felt envy, even while she was loving her.

"That was fun," said Ruth, coming back to her seat. "I think I *would* like to be in this operetta, after all."

"Oh, you will be," said Rosemary, but for herself she felt

only the quiet of despair. After today, she *knew* she was going to be left out.

On the way home she and Ruth decided that Franny Stapleton would probably be chosen for the lead. The operetta's heroine was Swiss, and Franny was blonde. On top of that, she had sung adequately and possessed a lot of charm and poise.

"I'd say she's the most poised girl in the ninth grade," said Ruth.

"Well, Ginger's pretty poised, too," said Rosemary.

"But she didn't try out," Ruth reminded her.

The girls turned the corner onto their own street. They were still discussing the operetta when suddenly there was an explosion of slamming doors. A boy of about nine or ten, carrying a grocery box in his arms, came tearing out of the Hauser house and ran down the street as if devils were after him. At least two devils were, because Bingo, barking and snarling, came right behind him, and then Mrs. Hauser herself, her transformation all askew, waving a broom. "Stop him!" she shrieked. "Stop, thief!"

Almost automatically, as the boy came by, Ruth stuck out her foot and he tripped over it. The box flew out of his hands, and for a few seconds he did a juggling act as he tried to regain his balance and catch the box at the same time. He managed to do it, but just barely, and then he was off again, but not before Rosemary had heard a kind of squawking noise coming from the box.

"Get him!" Mrs. Hauser screamed again. "He has your cat, Rosemary! Kidnapper!"

The brief pause in the boy's flight had given Bingo time

to catch up with him. He grabbed the boy's pant leg in his teeth and held on for dear life.

Across the street, Douglas was just emerging from his house, apparently on his way to an after-school job he had at a gas station. Noticing the excitement at his aunt's house, he shouted, "I'll catch him, Aunt Lottie!" and off he loped in pursuit, his long legs quickly diminishing the yards between him and the boy, who was dancing around trying to shake off Bingo. Bingo seemed to be enjoying the fuss as he growled and held on tighter.

Rosemary and Ruth stood there with their mouths wide open in astonishment, it had all happened so fast. Beside them, Mrs. Hauser gasped for breath.

"He—he—he walked right in," she sputtered. "He walked right into the house without knocking! I didn't even—didn't even see him until he was on his way out again, stuffing the cat into the box." She patted her transformation back into place and rearranged the waves in the hair. Her eyes were bright. She was having a wonderful time.

By now Douglas had caught the boy by the end of his coat and was bringing him back. The boy had still not relinquished his hold on the box, nor Bingo his hold on the boy. Douglas bent down and pried Bingo's jaws loose, then picked him up and held him. From there Bingo began to bark at the boy again.

"What do you want me to do with him?" Douglas asked, grinning. "Do you want me to call the police, Aunt Lottie?" Rosemary thought Douglas sounded just like John

Wayne. ("Wal, ma'am, what do you want me to do with this varmint, take him to the sheriff?")

"Maybe we ought to," said his aunt, with a fierce look at the boy. "Rosemary, is your cat all right?"

Rosemary took the box and lifted one corner of the lid. Instantly, a white paw, its wicked claws unsheathed, shot out. She closed the lid quickly. "He's all right," she said, and stuck her now bleeding finger into her mouth.

"I'm glad of that," said Mrs. Hauser, "but all the same, maybe we ought to call the police. Breaking and entering is a crime, you know." She fixed the boy with the kind of stern uncompromising stare that only the Mrs. Hausers of the world can successfully muster, and added with a grim smile, "Kidnapping is even worse."

The boy began to blubber; the tears made clean tracks down his small dirty face. "Please don't call the police!" he wailed. "I didn't mean anything by it."

"What do you mean you didn't mean anything?" Mrs. Hauser demanded.

"I was going to hold him for ransom for a little while, that's all. He's a rich cat, ain't he? I read it in my brother's school paper last night. My pa says cats ain't got any right to be rich when people are poor. But I wasn't going to ask for much, honest, maybe only two or three dollars."

"*Two or three dollars!*" Hands on hips, Mrs. Hauser stared at him as if she could not believe such infamy existed. "Call the police, Douglas."

"Oh, no, lady, please!" the boy whimpered. "I won't do it again. I promise."

"I should hope not!" Mrs. Hauser said, indignant.

"It's all right, Mrs. Hauser," Rosemary put in, trying to look serious. "I'm sure my mother wouldn't want us to put him in jail."

Mrs. Hauser pursed her lips. "Very well," she said. "It's up to you, of course. But," she added, glaring down at the boy, "you'd better not let me see you around here again. I'll be very hard on you the next time. You hear?"

"I hear," said the boy, tears still running down his cheeks. "Thanks, lady," he said to Rosemary, with a little half-sob, and when Douglas let go of him, he turned and, half running, half falling, fled from the scene of the crime.

Mrs. Hauser stared after him, shaking her head. "I never," she said, and she laughed softly.

Inside the box Thompson was clawing and complaining. "I'd better take him in," said Rosemary. "He's tearing the box apart."

"That cat," said Mrs. Hauser, "is more trouble than he's worth." Again she shook her head. "What a ruckus! I swear."

"Yes'm," said Rosemary. She rolled her eyes at Douglas and Ruth, then took Thompson back into the house.

14

Dearest Daddy,

Please forgive me for not writing before this, but I have been busy! Rehearsals have begun for the operetta, and I AM IN IT! I didn't think I would be, because I was so nervous the day I tried out, but Miss Alexander told me she and Miss Draper liked my voice, and also she had heard me sing often enough in class to know I could do it. I have the second lead, the part of an American girl visiting Switzerland with her mother and brother. Ruth plays the mother, and she is going to be very funny. She is supposed to be very scatterbrained and silly, and she is so good at it that she always has us all in stitches. Teddy Milhouse plays my brother. We have one big number together, called "Twirl Around Just So." It's a real catchy tune, and while we sing it we're supposed to be showing the Swiss kids how we dance in America. Teddy and I do a sort of jitterbug step. I like having Teddy as a partner. We've known each other all our lives, and we kind of bolster each other up. Remember how short he used to be? Well, he isn't now! The other day he was standing beside me, and I realized I didn't tower over him anymore. He is taller than I am.

Everybody thought Franny would get the lead, the part of the Swiss girl, but she didn't get a part at all. That was really surprising, but she says she doesn't care. I think she does, though. I would. Especially if everybody had been saying I would get something and then I didn't.

Margie Sorenson is playing the lead. I don't know her very well, because she's one of the kids who come to school on the bus, and they mostly have their click and we have ours. She's a little shy. But she's probably the best singer in the whole school.

Anyway, we are all really working hard, and it is fun.

I wish you could be home to see it. But I guess you won't be able to, will you?

Love and kisses,
Rosemary

P.S. I almost forgot the most AMAZING news of all. Mother said I could be the one to tell you about it. Thompson isn't rich anymore! The lawyer wrote to Mother just the other day and said that the estate is going to be settled in about a month and that she will get her bequest, with no strings attached. Isn't that wonderful? Thompson will be just a plain old cat again, and Mother will be the one who is rich! Mother said we had better not tell Mrs. Hauser about it, or she will make us get rid of Thompson. First of all, we don't think that would be fair to him, or for that matter to Aunt Milly, either. But second of all, we've discovered that we love the nasty beast.

Love again,
Rosemary

"Mother," said Rosemary, placing an envelope on top of the magazine she was using as a lap desk while writing to her father, "where do I address this one?"

"St. Louis," said her mother. "Here it is, in your father's last letter."

"Hey!" said Rosemary. "He's getting close to home! Oh, Mother, do you think he might come and see us? Do you think he might be here to actually see me in the operetta?"

"It's not probable, but it *is* possible," said her mother. She had been sitting in her chair, reading a mystery novel. Rosemary had been curled up on the couch, writing to her father with one ear tuned in on "Fibber McGee and Molly" on the radio. Anne Beedy's expression was thoughtful as she looked over at her daughter. Then she said, "Rosemary, turn the radio off; your program's over, anyway. I want to talk to you about something."

"Oh?" Rosemary reached over and cut off the commercial in midsentence. "What is it?" she asked. She thought her mother looked awfully serious. At the same time, though, she didn't seem unhappy or anything like that. But when her mother didn't answer right away, Rosemary added, "What did you want to tell me? You're making me nervous."

"Oh, it's nothing to be nervous about," said her mother.

"It's just that— Well, your father *is* coming home. But," she went on quickly before Rosemary could break in, "there are going to be some changes."

"Changes? Well, of course, there'll be changes. You do mean he's coming home to stay, don't you? Then we won't have to live here anymore, will we? We'll have a real home of our own again, isn't that right?"

"We will, but—but it won't be in Lynnfield." Her mother paused. "Let me start at the beginning. You know I've been very unhappy about this—this whole arrangement."

"Yes, I know that," said Rosemary. "I don't like having him away either."

"Your father knew how I—how we—felt. He knew about Paul too. I told him I was thinking of getting a divorce."

Rosemary felt a sudden panic. "But you're not, are you?"

Her mother smiled. "No, dear, I'm not. You know I haven't gone out with Paul for a long time. No, what is going to happen is: Your father has a job lined up. Not here, though. In Baltimore. We're going to move to Baltimore."

Rosemary stared at her. All she could feel was shock and disbelief. It didn't sound real. "Baltimore," she whispered. "That's in Maryland, isn't it?"

"Yes, it is."

Rosemary tried to visualize the map in her schoolbook. Baltimore was on the Chesapeake Bay, she was pretty sure. It was a city. She had never lived in a city. A thrill went through her. That might be exciting. It was certainly something new. "When?" she asked. "When are we going?"

"In a couple of months."

"Two months! That's April. . . . The operetta is in March. . . . Well, that's OK."

"Oh, yes. You won't miss the operetta. Your father is planning to leave the band in March, and then he'll go right to Baltimore to look for an apartment for us. He ought to be back here by April, and meantime, you and I can get started with the packing up."

"Yes . . ." Rosemary's voice trailed off. The excitement she had felt initially at the thought of living in a city was still there, churning up inside her, presenting all sorts of possibilities, but now other feelings were beginning to overtake it. All at once she realized that her familiar world, everything she took for granted, was in danger of disappearing. With the thought came a terrible sense of loss. "Mother," she faltered, "will . . . this be . . . forever?"

"Rosemary, darling, forever is a long time."

"But . . . as far as you know it is. Isn't it? I mean, once we leave here, we're not coming back?"

Her mother's eyes were solemn. "No, Rosemary, we're not. We'll be starting a new life in Baltimore."

"But my friends! I can't leave my friends!"

"Rosemary, I'll be leaving my friends too."

"I know, but—" But it wasn't the same, Rosemary thought. Her mother was leaving her friends of her own volition; she, Rosemary, would not be. She was being manipulated, forced into a break with her whole past, just because it suited someone else. Oh, it wasn't fair. She had no say in the matter at all. Suddenly the feelings of personal grievance she felt about all that were overwhelming.

Her mother moved closer to her and put her arms around her. "Look, Rosemary, you don't *have* to go. You'll still have grandparents here, and they love you. If you want to stay with them, you can, you know. And Aunt Jo will still be here in town. You're not really being forced into anything. . . . Would you rather stay here with Gramma and Grampa? Is that what you prefer to do?"

"I don't kn-o-ow!" Rosemary wailed.

"Well, think about it. Nothing has to be decided tonight —or tomorrow—or even next week. You have until April to make up your mind. Honey, don't cry. Please. You don't have to go."

"Don't you and Daddy want me with you?" Rosemary sniffled and wiped her nose with the back of her hand.

"Of course we do! You're our only child. But we want you to be happy too, and if you'll be happier staying here, then you should."

"But," said Rosemary, "won't you be lonely without me?"

"I'd miss you, naturally. I'd rather have you there. But the fact is, I won't be around all the time, Rosemary. I intend to get a job once we're settled. We may need the extra money for a while. And, besides that, I've discovered these last few months that I like working."

"I see." Rosemary was silent. She felt better, but not much. She still felt tearful, sad to her bones about many things. Either way, whatever she decided, nothing was ever going to be the same. "What's it like?" she asked. "Baltimore, I mean."

"I've never been there," said her mother. "But I've heard

there are rows and rows of houses, all with white steps."

"Can you see the Chesapeake Bay from there?"

"I don't know. . . . But I think the weather is hotter than here—in the summer, that is."

"I suppose so." Rosemary sighed. "Well, I'll think about it," she said.

"Meanwhile, I'll tell Gramma and Grandpa that you may be moving in with them. They'll be delighted, of course. But," her mother continued, "I'll tell them they're not to influence you in any way. This must be *your* decision, Rosemary."

Rosemary nodded unhappily. Then she picked up her fountain pen and the letter she had written to her father. "P.P.S.," she wrote. "Mother just told me that we—that is, you—are moving to Baltimore in April. I may be going with you. On the other hand, I may not. I haven't made up my mind yet. When I do, I will let you know."

For a while, despite her sorrow and mixed feelings, Rosemary thought that her mother had handed her a wonderful gift: the opportunity to decide for herself about something that was bound to affect her profoundly. For a while, she walked about her town and saw it with new eyes. Everything took on importance: the ivy growing up the library stones, the special feeling of the movie theater where she and Ruth had spent so many Saturdays of their life, the yellow bricks of the school and the view of the mountains behind the athletic field, the narrow main street of the town winding past the courthouse to the shopping area with all its familiar stores.

She did not tell her friends, not even Ruth, right away. She knew they would urge her to stay, and she did not want them to affect her decision.

If she, Rosemary, went away, she might never see any of them again, and she would never see Douglas either. Oh, she could come back on visits, she supposed, but that wouldn't be the same thing. *Never* again. "Quoth the Raven, 'Nevermore!'" What a terrible word.

But if she stayed here, if she didn't go, she would be separated from her mother, from whom she had never been separated, and she would continue to be separated from her father, after all these months of being apart. What was more, she would miss out on a new experience; she would not be a part of the adventure that was coming.

No, it was an awful responsibility having to make up her own mind. Her mother hadn't done her any favor by leaving it all up to her. Being pushed around, told what to do, was aggravating, but how much worse it was, she realized now, to have to push yourself, one way or the other, when you wanted both things and yet didn't want either.

And when her mother asked her, a week or so later, whether she had come to any decision, Rosemary merely groaned. "One day I think one way, and the next day I think the other. I hope this is the last decision I ever have to make!"

Her mother smiled a little sadly. "I'm afraid that's one wish that will never come true. Life is full of decisions, and sometimes, no matter how careful we are, we make the wrong ones. I'm sorry, honey, but it's just as well you're getting some practice now."

And so the days went by, and Rosemary still did not make up her mind. Three years of junior high were winding to a close, and there was much talk about "next year when we're in high school!" It was talk in which Rosemary did not join, because she kept wondering, But will I be there too? Or will I be in some other school I've never even heard of? Her secret made her feel like an outsider.

There was the operetta too, of course. Rosemary loved the rehearsals, which were teaching her something she had not known before: The *work* involved in a show was the important, the enjoyable thing; the glory was only second. Was that why her father liked being in a dance band? It certainly wasn't making him famous, so the work itself must be enough. How was he going to feel, she wondered, after he had given it up and taken on a just-plain job in Baltimore?

Her mind flitted uncomfortably away from that thought; it was something she could do nothing about. No, she would think about the operetta. It was changing her in lots of ways. For instance, the operetta itself was so real that it was helping her to stop daydreaming. For a while she had often caught herself backsliding, but lately, she noticed, she was daydreaming less and less. In its place, she realized, she had become very aware of herself. She was aware of how she walked and talked, of how she appeared to other people. Reality—that was what was important, she thought, and so, when she walked down the street these days, she no longer made up stories about being someone else. No, she stood off mentally and watched herself, Rosemary Beedy, walking down the street.

One night was all the cast of the operetta had to look forward to after all their work. But that night, when at last it came, held for them almost enough excitement. The school librarian did the makeup, and when she was through, everybody seemed to be in Technicolor. Rosemary, who had never used makeup before, was amazed at how exotic she looked. Maybe, from now on, she would use some—a little lipstick—if her mother did not object.

Backstage all was in chaos, with the large chorus, the main actors, and three harried teachers all getting in one another's way. The air was electric. Peering through a crack in the curtain just before the overture, Rosemary saw the people filing in. Never had the auditorium been so filled. Her mother was out there, she knew, and her grandparents, and Aunt Jo, and her other two aunts (also her father's sisters) who lived out of town, not to mention Mr. and Mrs. Hauser and Malvina. They were all rooting for her, of course, but that didn't help much. Her whole body felt tingly, as if small electric currents were shooting through her, and when the school orchestra, slightly out of tune, struck up the overture, she was sure she was going to pass out.

Ruth, who had been the last to be made up, appeared at her side. She had on a wig and one of her mother's dresses, and her natural curves had been greatly maximized. She looked so much like Mrs. Hauser that Rosemary giggled.

"Break a leg," Ruth said.

"What?"

"That's what they say in show business. Didn't you know that? They think it's bad luck to say 'Good luck.'"

"Oh," said Rosemary. "Well, break a leg yourself. Are you scared?"

"Only pleasantly so." Pursing up her face, Ruth spoke in the high-pitched voice of the character she was playing.

Rosemary giggled again. Ruth was going to steal the show, so no one would notice her, anyway. She was rather glad of that, in a way; it made her feel less nervous.

Just then there was a lot of excited whispering backstage; Miss Alexander, looking frazzled, said, "Quiet, everybody," and gave an order. The boy in charge of the curtain slowly pulled it open. "Go on, go on!" Miss Alexander whispered frantically, and the chorus filed onstage. After much shuffling of feet and jockeying for position, they broke into a lively song about Switzerland. The operetta had begun.

Rosemary suffered one bad moment right after she went onstage. She knew her part backward and forward and every other way, but all of a sudden her mind was a complete blank. She couldn't say anything. She stood right there onstage, her mouth slowly opening, her panic rising.

Teddy, the boy who was playing her brother, nudged her. "Could you tell us the way to Herr Schmidt's inn?" he muttered out of the side of his mouth.

Shooting him a quick, grateful glance, Rosemary said the line. Immediately her memory came back, and for the rest of the operetta she was all right. Even the solo singing was easy now, because she had lines to say before she sang, which helped her get into it.

As everybody had suspected, Ruth was the big hit of the show. The audience loved her. But Rosemary felt that her own song with Teddy went well, and when she heard the applause the two of them got as, behind them, the chorus took up the refrain, a thrill of joy and accomplishment went through her.

At the very end, though, when all of the cast and chorus stood onstage for the very last time, holding hands and swaying to the music and singing the finale, Rosemary had to fight back the tears. It was all over: all the fun of rehearsals, this wonderful scary night itself . . . even junior high (almost). But not old friendships! No. Tonight had helped her make up her mind. She wasn't leaving; she was never going to leave. She was going to stay here in Lynnfield forever.

15

April, spring, and Rosemary's father arrived almost simultaneously. Even the terrible news that in Europe Hitler had invaded Denmark and Norway could not dim her happiness and sense of well-being. Europe was very far away. Here at home buds were showing their green, and grass was growing in the fields and front lawns. In the backyard Mr. Hauser's daffodils were a sunny yellow all along the back fence, and purple hyacinths bordering the walk sent up such a fragrance that Rosemary could sometimes smell them in her room at night. She felt overcome by romance and strange longings and a sudden unfamiliar restlessness. Seeing Douglas sitting thoughtfully on his front steps, his head against the post, she wondered what he was thinking about. It hadn't occurred to her before that boys might daydream too, and she was suffused with such feelings of love that she sat down and wrote a poem about him.

The next afternoon, a Saturday, she was coming out of the Lynnfield Palace with Ruth when she saw Douglas walking along hand in hand with a very pretty girl with short, dark, curly hair—the girl of the skating rink. Rosemary gave a gasp and ducked back into the theater. With a low moan, she turned her back to the street and pressed herself sideways into the wall.

"So Mitch has a girl," Ruth said, her tone of voice irritatingly practical. "So what? What did you expect?"

"I don't have to look at it, do I? Oh, Ruth, I wouldn't want him to see me looking at them." She peered around furtively. "Tell me when they're gone," she whispered.

Ruth went to the door. "They *are* gone. They're walking up toward the Esso station where Mitch works."

Cautiously Rosemary left the theater with Ruth. Her heart ached unbearably. Suspecting something, and finding it really was true, were two different things.

When she got back home, she took out the poem she had written about Douglas and reread it. It sounded so sappy now that she almost gagged, and she tore it into tiny pieces and flushed the pieces down the toilet.

A few days later her father came home. She and her mother went to the train to meet him, and Rosemary was really surprised at how nervous both of them were—although they didn't discuss their feelings with each other. Her mother was wearing white gloves with a button at the wrist, and as they stood on the platform waiting for the train, she noticed that her mother kept buttoning and unbuttoning the gloves without being aware of what she was doing. Rosemary herself wondered what she was going to say to her father, and when the train puffed in and screeched to a stop, blowing out steam, her heart was in her mouth.

Her father descended from the train at the other end of the platform. Anne Beedy recognized him first. She made a breathy little sound and ran toward him. Rosemary got an impression of small violence from the way they went into each other's arms, and she held back, turning her face away. Then, in a little while, they were beside her and her father was saying, "Rosemary! Let me look at you." He held her by the shoulders. "Good Lord! I hardly recognize you. You've really grown!"

"Yes," said Rosemary. Shyly, she held up her face to be kissed.

But he hugged her first, then kissed her. "When I went away you were still a little girl."

"I'm not a little girl anymore, Daddy," she told him. But even as she spoke he had turned away from her again and was giving all his attention to her mother, as if he could not believe they were together again.

Rosemary trailed behind them carrying one of the suitcases, as they walked, her father with his free arm around her mother's shoulders, toward the taxi stand. In the taxi, too, he sat with his arm around her, her hand in his, in the back seat, while Rosemary sat in front with the driver. She felt more than a little left out. Who was he, this stranger who had dropped into the middle of their placid life and who was so anxious to change everything? She did not know him. He was not anything like the father who had left home. She had wanted him to come back, but now she found herself wishing he would go away again. Why not? She and her mother had been getting along perfectly well. Now that she thought about it, even Paul had not seemed like such a threat. She knew her mother had told him about Paul. Probably that was why he had decided to come home.

Rosemary continued to sulk for the rest of the evening. She knew she was sulking, but she could not help herself. Anyway, her parents did not seem to notice, they were so wrapped up in each other. Oh, her father did try to show an interest in her, but she had the uncomfortable sense that he did not know what to say to her either. His eyes were shy as he asked her about school and about the operetta. Then he tried to make a fuss over Thompson, and Thompson bit his thumb.

"We're not taking this cat with us, are we?" her father asked as her mother daubed Mercurochrome over the bite.

"We certainly are!"

"To Baltimore?" Rosemary picked up Thompson and cuddled him in her arms, a familiarity he would occasionally put up with from her or her mother. "I thought he'd go to Gramma's with me."

"Now, honey, you know your grandmother doesn't like cats."

They were all in the kitchen preparing a late supper. Rosemary was setting the table. "Not even her own dead sister's cat?" she asked. "I think Gramma might make an exception with Thompson."

"A cat's a cat. She doesn't make any exceptions," said her

mother. Then she added, "Rosemary, don't walk around the table with the cat in your arms."

Frowning, Rosemary set Thompson on the floor. It seemed as if *everything* was being taken away from her.

After supper Rosemary got ready to listen to her favorite radio programs, but her mother said she and Rosemary's father preferred to talk. Of course, they had plans to make, didn't they? And they wanted to be alone, too. Rosemary sensed that strongly.

Well, she didn't want to be where she wasn't wanted. "I think I'll go to bed," she said glumly, and when nobody asked her to stay, she gathered up Thompson and left the room.

After soaking in the tub for a while, she curled up on her bed with her movie star scrapbook. Lately she had stopped collecting William Holden and gone back to collecting Tyrone Power, who had been her earlier and longer-standing favorite. Besides, she was always getting William Holden mixed up with Douglas who, after all, was much closer and more real than any Hollywood star, except—she frowned —she'd rather not think about that girl she had seen him with on Saturday.

Rosemary thoughtfully cut a picture out of a magazine and pasted it into the scrapbook. Then she rolled the loose scraps of paper into a ball and tossed the ball on the floor for Thompson to play with. He batted it around a little bit, then lost interest and jumped onto the bed, right into the middle of the scrapbook.

"Watch out!" said Rosemary. She lifted him off the scrapbook and closed it before he could do any real damage. "Honestly, you're a pest," she told him. "I'm glad you're going to Baltimore with them. I'll be well rid of you."

Thompson sat regally at the foot of the bed, staring at her. He looked awfully pretty, she thought, as he closed his green eyes at her, then opened them again.

"Even you are going to leave me," she said dully, her voice tinged with tears. She swung her legs around to the floor and placed the scrapbook back on top of the bookcase. Then she opened the window, got into bed, and turned off the light. Outside an April shower had begun; she could hear the raindrops plopping down between the houses. They smelled of the earth and of damp sidewalks. At her feet Thompson circled around several times, then curled up heavily, taking up his usual inordinate amount of room. Over the sound of the rain she could hear him purring loudly, but she felt very much alone.

In the morning Rosemary rushed down the hallway to the kitchen, feeling, as usual, a little late, but as she rounded the corner by Malvina's room she stopped short. Her mother and father were already in the kitchen talking.

"I'll admit it seemed selfish," her father was saying, "but I was only trying to make a living. I thought I was doing the best thing."

"I realize that," she heard her mother murmur, "but it wasn't the best thing for any of us."

"You weren't really serious about that—that—Paul, were you? I couldn't believe it when you told me what you did. Anne, if I thought that, I—"

"I was flattered, I guess," her mother put in. "But I wasn't in love with him. You *know* that, Eddie. But . . . you were so far away. I felt you were never coming back."

"Well, I'm here," he said harshly.

"Yes," she said, "you're here."

They were silent, and Rosemary, suddenly aware that she was eavesdropping again, turned to flee. But then she heard her father say, "You've done a great job with Rosemary, honey. She's turning out well. I'm proud of her."

"You'd have been prouder," said her mother, "if you'd seen her in that operetta. Oh, Eddie, she was so dear, and a lot of people mentioned to me what a sweet voice she has."

Hmm, thought Rosemary. Then she went back to her room, turned, and stomped back down the hall, so they would think she had just arrived.

"Hi," she said. "I'd better eat breakfast and run. I'm late. My alarm isn't working right, Mother." She put two pieces of bread in the toaster and mixed herself a glass of Cocomalt and milk, her usual breakfast. While she was waiting for the toast, she got an orange out of the refrigerator for her lunch, spread two more slices of bread with peanut butter, and slapped them together.

"We'd better make arrangements with the mover today," her mother was saying to her father.

Rosemary whirled around. "Mover?" she said. "When— when are you leaving?"

"Why, in a week," said her father. "That's when I start my new job."

"Oh-h," said Rosemary, and just stood there. It was true

her mother had started packing a few nonessential things, but there had been no sense of hurry about it.

Behind her, her mother buttered her toast for her and put it on a plate. "Sit down and eat," she said.

"What about my furniture?" Rosemary asked. "My bed and dressing table—and my books and scrapbooks and things."

"Well, your personal things will go with you to your grandmother's. I'm sure you'll want them with you," her mother explained. "But the furniture—I guess that will have to go with us to Baltimore. I assume," she added wistfully, "you'll be coming down to visit us occasionally."

"Oh, Mother!" Stricken, Rosemary stared at her.

"You've got to remember," her mother continued, "your grandparents won't have room for any extra furniture, their house is so small, and they already have a place for you to sleep."

Rosemary nodded. "The spare room," she said. She could see the room in her mind's eye: very small, like her own room now, only not as cozy, not as personal. Her grandmother kept her sewing machine in there, and the tiny closet was filled with her grandparents' out-of-season clothing. A narrow bed filled the only available corner for it and was seldom slept in, except on the ever-more-rare visits of her grandfather's aging sister. A print called *Stag at Bay*, in a dime-store frame, hung over the bed. It was so depressing that Rosemary could never bear to look at it, and she hoped she'd be allowed to take it down and replace it with a picture of Tyrone Power.

Rosemary stirred her Cocomalt mixture, but she

couldn't pick it up and swallow it, her throat felt so constricted.

"Mother, I—" She stopped, and started again. "I—"

"You what?" said her mother.

And then Rosemary said what she had known all along, deep in her heart, she was going to say. "Mother, I want to go with you!" She put her head down on the table and sobbed.

"But, baby," her father crooned at her, "don't you know that's what we've wanted all along?" She heard him get up from his chair and come over to her and felt his arms go around her and draw her close. And suddenly he was once more the father she remembered, the father she had written letters to—not the aloof stranger who had got off the train the day before.

"I didn't think you wanted me with you," she sobbed.

"Now, Rosemary, that's not true," said her mother, and she sounded irritable. "You said you didn't want to leave your friends."

"I don't," Rosemary admitted thickly, "but I don't want to lose you either, and—and, anyway, I don't want to miss all the fun. Even—even *Thompson* is going!" she wailed, and she couldn't understand why, suddenly, her parents laughed so hard they had to wipe their eyes.

At any rate, it was settled, she thought. She was going with them, after all. She felt as if she had voluntarily turned her world upside down, but for some reason she felt better about it than she had ever thought she would.

16

At lunchtime Rosemary's sandwich was so dry she could hardly eat it; she had forgotten to stir the peanut butter when the jar was new, and this morning there had been nothing left but the dry stuff on the bottom. However, she worried the sandwich down and listened silently as Ruth talked about *Gone With the Wind*. The picture was starting a whole week's run in Lynnfield the following day, and she and Rosemary had bought tickets for the opening night.

"You haven't said a word. Aren't you excited?" said Ruth. "Sometimes you try to act so blasé, Rosemary."

Rosemary took a swallow of chocolate milk, and the last blob of peanut butter reluctantly went down. "I am—so excited," she said. "And I'm not blasé. I am merely choking to death."

"Want me to hit you on the back?"

"No!" said Rosemary.

"My brother and his girl said it was unbelievable."

"What was?"

"*Gone With the Wind,* stupid! What have we been talking about? They saw it in Pittsburgh."

"I can hardly wait," said Rosemary. "I can't get it into my head yet that we're finally going to see it after all the publicity." Soberly she began peeling her orange. "Ruth . . ." she said.

"What?"

"Remember I told you my parents were going to Baltimore to live after my father came home?"

"Uh-huh."

"And I said I was going to go and live with my grandparents?"

Ruth nodded.

"Well, my father came home yesterday, and he says he has to leave for Baltimore in a week, and— Well, I'm going to go with them."

Ruth's eyes grew big and round. "What are you talking about? For how long?"

"To stay. I've changed my mind. I'm going to Baltimore with my parents."

The incomprehension on Ruth's face changed to anger. "Why, you dirty stinker!" she shouted. "What are you telling me that now for? Spoiling the day! Spoiling tomorrow night! What do you mean you're going to Baltimore? You don't have to go. You can stay here if you want."

Rosemary shrank down inside her shoulders. "But I don't want," she said, grimacing. She peered around and saw that the other kids in the cafeteria were staring at them. "Don't you understand? I want to be with my parents. Besides, it'll be fun."

"Fun? Phooey!" Ruth exclaimed. "A fine friend you are. You're not a friend at all, Rosemary Beedy. Well, I don't give a darn whether you go or not. In fact, I'm glad you're going! I don't ever want to see your stupid face again." Ruth got up so fast she knocked her chair over. Leaving it on the floor, she swished out of the cafeteria with her nose in the air. Everyone turned and stared after her in curiosity.

Rosemary went over and picked up the chair. She felt embarrassed. Worse, she felt sorry. She hadn't expected Ruth to take it so hard. She was really surprised. Somehow, she had thought that all the hurt, all the missing would be on her side alone.

Ruth avoided Rosemary for the rest of the day, and for most of the next day too. However, they had bought their seats for *Gone With the Wind* ahead of time, and those seats were situated side by side.

Rosemary got to the theater first that night. When Ruth arrived she didn't say anything to Rosemary or even look at her. She sat down and started looking at her program.

"Hi, Ruth."

Ruth pretended not to hear. She turned the pages of her program with intense interest. Rosemary sighed and did the same, but she hoped Ruth would come around. They had looked forward to this movie for so long, it would be a shame to spoil it.

But just then the lights dimmed and the picture began. The words *Gone With the Wind* unrolled before their eyes, and the music—the music—

"Oh, Ruth!" Rosemary breathed. "I can't stand it!"

"Me neither!" Ruth whispered. Her eyes were riveted to the screen. There was no longer any need to talk, nor were they able to.

When intermission arrived, they turned to each other and began to speak once more, tentatively at first, in the polite, desultory fashion they always assumed after an argument, but at least, Rosemary thought, they were talking. They rather distantly discussed the personalities of the actors and the merits of the cast, but gradually their delight with the movie began to bubble over.

"Oh, Ruth!" Rosemary said. "Didn't you love the scene where the war started—you know, when Scarlett walked up the staircase? That was so dramatic."

"Yes, but I think that train station with all the wounded lying there was even more dramatic," said Ruth.

Rosemary nodded. "I cried when the casualty lists came out, didn't you?"

"Yes," said Ruth.

The movie came on again. The Civil War finally came to an end, and Scarlett eventually married Rhett. With the death of Bonnie, both Rosemary and Ruth burst into tears. They could not stop crying. They glanced at each other and got the giggles, but that only made them slightly hysterical. They kept on crying until the picture ended.

People got up and filed out of the theater, but Rosemary and Ruth continued to sit there. Rosemary blew her nose. Then Ruth said in a shaky voice, "That's the best movie ever made."

"Oh, yes," Rosemary breathed. "Oh, I wish I were Vivien Leigh."

"Yeah," Ruth whispered, "and married to Clark Gable."

"She isn't really married to him."

"I know that!" Ruth said.

"Tomorrow's Saturday. Let's come again," said Rosemary.

"All right," said Ruth.

"Do you want to come to my house at eleven thirty?"

"Frankly, my dear," said Ruth, "I don't give a damn. But I will!"

The week went fast. There was *Gone With the Wind* to see again on Saturday; there was dinner at her grandparents' on Sunday, evening visits to her out-of-town aunts. The rest of the time was taken up by packing. There, too, Rosemary found she had some hard decisions to make. Her mother had told her to get rid of all her junk, everything she didn't honestly want, and so she went through her possessions in a mood from which all sentimentality had been removed—she hoped. She finally decided that she would never again read her Nancy Drew books or want to look through her early, less discriminating movie-star scrapbooks or play with her old paper dolls and beat-up-looking Shirley Temple doll. She piled them all to one side, and if they seemed forlorn waiting there while she packed the rest of her things, she did not look at them and she did not give in.

They were to leave on Saturday, so Friday was her last day at Lincoln Junior High. At the end of each class that day the teacher stopped her on the way out of the room and said good-bye, and when the day itself ended, her homeroom teacher and all her friends had a little ceremony in which they gave her a pretty scarf and told her how much they were going to miss her. By that time Rosemary could not hold back the tears and was deeply regretting her decision to leave.

Before going home she had to go to the principal's office to pick up her records so she could take them to her new school. For a minute or two he held them back from her and just stood looking down at her.

"Rosemary, I hate to give these to you," he said. "I'm sure you'll be coming back."

She shook her head. "No," she told him. "I'm never coming back." And as she walked out of the school later with the envelope in her hand, she wondered how she could have been so positive, so definite. It was possible, of course, that she would return, but for some reason, she just knew she wouldn't.

Ruth came down that evening, but everything was upset. The whole family was there, and there was no place to sit, and conversation was difficult, so Ruth asked Rosemary to walk her home.

They left the house, walking slowly so as to prolong these last moments together. Ruth didn't say anything at first. Then, "Stay," she begged, her voice breaking. "It isn't too late. You can still stay."

But the trouble was it was too late now. It was as if Rosemary were on a train that was going faster and faster. She didn't know where it was going exactly, but it was too late to jump off.

"I can't," she whispered. "I wish you understood."

"I don't understand," Ruth said. "I'll just be glad when you're gone, that's all."

"Well, I like that!"

"No, I mean it. I wish you were going to stay, but since you won't, I just wish you'd go. I don't like saying good-bye, and I hate this hanging about and feeling in-between."

"I know what you mean," said Rosemary. "I feel the same way. But anyway, I'll come back and visit in the summer. You want me to, don't you?"

"I guess so," said Ruth. She thought about that for a minute. "Maybe someday I'll visit you, too. Actually, I wouldn't mind seeing Baltimore. It's right now that I can't stand."

"Me neither," said Rosemary.

When they reached Ruth's house, Ruth ran up the steps as if she weren't going to say anything more, but at the door she paused and said abruptly, "I'll be down in the morning to see you off."

But in the morning Rosemary was afraid Ruth wasn't going to make it. The truck with the furniture had already left, and the 1935 Plymouth her father had bought for the trip was piled high, with parents in the front seat and Rosemary and Thompson, who was staring dejectedly out through the mesh door of his old carrier, in the back, along with all the luggage that wouldn't fit in the trunk. Mr. and Mrs. Hauser and Bingo, Malvina and the lady from next door were all standing around the car when Ruth ran down the street, still looking half asleep.

"Rosemary," she gasped, "I was afraid you'd be gone!"

"No, I'm still here."

Ruth was carrying a large used manila envelope from her father's business. She handed it to Rosemary through the car window. "Here," she said. "My five best pictures of Tyrone Power are in there. And two of Clark Gable." She stuck out her lower lip. "I really had to fight with myself to give up those last two, but I want you to have them." She backed away from the window trying, unsuccessfully, to look nonchalant.

"Thanks," said Rosemary. "I'll write to you, Ruth. Will you write to me?"

"Oh, sure." Ruth waved her hand airily. Then she added, "Well, I really have to go home now, Rosemary." She paused. "Gum-bye," she said. Then she turned and ran back up the street as fast as she could go.

Heart-sore, Rosemary sat back in her seat. She had been right all along about not wanting to leave her friends, and losing Ruth was the worst thing that could happen to her. After all, you didn't find a best friend every day. Today was Saturday, too—movie day. Would Ruth go alone? For years neither one of them had ever missed a Saturday, unless she was ill—until today.

Oh, maybe she shouldn't go to Baltimore! It wasn't too late. . . .

Her father glanced back at her with a look of uncertainty on his face. "Rosemary?" When she didn't answer right away, he cleared his throat as if in sympathy, then gunned the car's motor.

"Hey, wait a minute!" someone yelled.

Douglas had come out of his house and was running

across the street. He shoved a package done up in tissue paper through the window at Rosemary.

"What's this?"

"Don't open it now. Open it later," he said. His curly auburn hair flopped over his forehead as he bent down and peered in at her. "Hey, Rosemary," he said, "I'm going to miss you. You're the craziest girl I've ever known. It's been real interesting knowing you."

"Ha!" said Rosemary, for lack of any other reply. His attitude was far from romantic; he might have been talking to another boy. But then, as Ruth would say, what did she expect? He already had a girl. And he had never thought of her that way. He had only been accommodating his aunt all along.

"Well, I've got to go to work," he said. "Good-bye, Mr. and Mrs. Beedy. So long, Rosemary. Good luck."

"So long," she said, and she waved halfheartedly, consumed by her growing sense of loss. But he had already disappeared.

And then, inevitably, in the midst of farewells and cautions to drive carefully from their neighbors on the sidewalk, her father turned the car out into the street, and they started on their journey. "Good-bye! Good-bye!" she heard them say, but they soon left everyone behind. They drove past Ruth's house, but she was nowhere to be seen, and her house presented a blank facade to the street.

Tears stung Rosemary's eyes, but she did not look back, just sat there stiffly, Douglas's package in her lap. They passed the Wakely house, where for one brief moment he had held her in his arms. Then, instead of turning left toward her grandparents' house, they turned right toward Route 40—Route 40, which would take them to Baltimore and a new life.

"I wonder," said Rosemary, "if I'll ever see Douglas again."

"Maybe, when you come back to visit this summer," suggested her mother.

"Maybe," said Rosemary, but without conviction.

"What's in the package he gave you?"

"I don't know." Rosemary untied the string and removed the tissue paper. Inside was a cardboard box. Inside the box was a toy gun, not the one he had taken from her years before, but a brand-new shiny black one.

"For heaven's sake," said her mother. "What's that? A cap pistol?"

"Yes." Rosemary's fingers tightened around the gun, and she brought it up to her cheek.

Her mother gave a little snort. "That's an odd present."

"No, it isn't," Rosemary told her. "It's just what you'd expect him to give the craziest girl he's ever known." And in his eyes, she thought ruefully, that was all she had ever been.

Now, at last, she did turn and look back out of the car's rear window, but all she could see were the less familiar streets on the outskirts of Lynnfield. Douglas was gone, Ruth was gone, everything was gone. But she had made her decision, and there was no point in beating her breast about it. From now on her life would take an entirely new direction . . . for she had changed the future.

17

South along Route 40 and into the mountains, past Fort Necessity, the site of many childhood jaunts; through Addison and past the house that had once belonged to her paternal grandparents. They were gone now, and the house had been sold several years before, but the barn where she had once played in the summer was still there, and so was the apple orchard, soon to be in bloom, where she and a second cousin had climbed trees in their tomboy moments and held doll tea parties in their ladylike ones. All of it was long over with now, except for this one last trip into the past for her to say good-bye.

And good-bye also to what you might still call the present, she thought, as over the Mason and Dixon line they went into Maryland—into the South, she told herself with a thrill, as visions of Scarlett and Rhett danced in her head. Over Keysers Ridge and into the future they drove. Pangs of homesickness assailed her as they penetrated deeper into this new state—home was beginning to seem very far away —but curiosity about what lay beyond each turn in the road, about what her new life would be like was stronger right now than homesickness.

At Frostburg her father said, "My mother was born here."

"I didn't know that!" Rosemary exclaimed. "That kind of makes us Southerners, then, doesn't it?"

"We-l-l, not exactly. I don't think she lived here very long."

But Rosemary clung to the thought. She felt now that she belonged in Maryland, a little bit.

They had lunch in Cumberland, and Rosemary took Thompson, who had fallen asleep for want of anything else to do, out of his carrier and let him walk around the inside of the car. Then they went on. Hagerstown—they were over the mountains now—Frederick. Soon they would be in Baltimore, and the future would begin.

Dear Ruth,

I have been here a whole day and night, and already I miss you horribly. I can't *believe* I can't go outside and walk up the street and find you at your house the same as always. But your house is very far away now, and it has all happened so suddenly.

I will tell you about our new apartment. Daddy says it is just temporary until we find something in the suburbs. He didn't have much time to look for a place, and this is what he came up with. Actually, it isn't bad. It's near downtown Baltimore on a wide street with a kind of park, with statues, down the middle. The apartment is on the third floor. It has a dining room at one end and a living room at the other. In between is a long hall with the kitchen, bathroom, and two bedrooms leading off it. Thompson was very unhappy here at first, and awfully jumpy and nervous. Then suddenly tonight he discovered that he liked the hall, and he began running up and down it sideways with his tail in the air and a wild look in his eyes.

Tomorrow I start at my new school, and you'll never guess what it is. A Catholic all-girls school. Mother got that idea in her head from a friend of hers back home, who said I'd learn a lot more there. Mother didn't spring it on me, though, until after we got here. She says she's going to pay the tuition out of Thompson's money, that bequest from Aunt Milly, until she gets a job.

I don't know what to think about it. I'll write and tell you after I've been there. Meanwhile, I hope you will write to me and tell me all about *everything*.

> *Your undying friend,*
> *Rosemary*

Dear Ruth,

Thanks for your letter. Of *course* I will save it. I will save all your letters if you will save all of mine. And if you see Douglas, give him a big kiss for me. Ha, ha.

Yes, I started at the new school the Monday after we got here, and it certainly was strange. It still seems strange to me. The nuns wear big pointy white hats that make them look like enormous birds, and the girls all wear uniforms—the same thing everywhere you look—dark blue jumpers and white blouses, and each class walks in a line from room to room with a leader at the front and a follower at the back, just like prisoners or something. And not a boy in sight, or a man teacher, except for one priest who comes once a week and gives the senior girls instruction in Catholic Marriage and another priest, a tall gangly one, who leads the school in singing, or I guess chanting, a mass in Gregorian chant. I have been excused from that, because they're going to sing the mass at the Cathedral next Sunday, so I just sit in the back of the auditorium and listen.

My classes are all mixed up too, because I have had some things my class hasn't had, and vice versa. Because of that I have one free period a day. I'm supposed to spend it in the library studying, but I've never gotten there, not once. The first time I started to go to it, I was walking past the empty auditorium when I heard a "Psst," and saw a finger beckoning me inside. I went in, and there was a girl at the end of the finger. She was sort of short and chubby with short red hair and a wicked gleam in her eye. She doesn't look like you, Ruth, but something about her reminds me of you. I think that's why I liked her right away.

She told me her name is Mary Anne Kelly, but that everyone calls her Kelly, and that she is new too (she has been in the school about a month—her family moved in from the country to be nearer her father's work). She said she has never been to study hall since she's been here. Instead, she always comes to the auditorium and plays the piano backstage (she studies piano at Peabody), and in all that time no one has ever missed her or caught her in the auditorium. But she said she'd be glad to have some company, and so that's what I've been doing.

It's been a lot of fun hiding out from the nuns, and

we've become real good friends. I never thought I'd make a friend this fast. She invited me out to her house last Saturday, and we rode bikes, hers and one she borrowed, and on Sunday we went to the movies. Her favorite movie actor is Don Ameche. I don't know why, because he never gets the girl or anything, but she thinks he's wonderful. And next Saturday afternoon we're going to see a real stage play! Kelly's father works for the *Sun* and he gets free tickets, so it won't cost anything. Next time I write I'll tell you how it was.

When is the ninth grade going to make its traditional visit to Lynnfield High? Just think, *I* got into high school before any of you.

Please write.

Love,
Rosemary

Dear Ruth,

I do *not* like Kelly better than I do you.
And I am *not* bragging.
If that is the way you feel, I won't write to you anymore.

Yours truly,
Rosemary Beedy

Dear Ruth,

I'm sorry, and I do want to write to you. You are still my best friend and the person I love best in all the world except for my family. It's true I didn't have to come here with my parents, but I did, and sometimes I wish I didn't. Sometimes I get so homesick I could die.

But my new friends have helped a lot. Besides Kelly, there is a girl with long pigtails named Bernadette, who is a real artist. She goes to the Maryland Institute on Saturdays and studies how to do it.

That is one of the advantages of living in a city. There are all kinds of places you can go to study things. . . .

Rosemary paused. She had better not say that. It sounded like bragging again. She would have to start the letter over.

Still, she did not want to do that now. It was nearly five thirty, and Rosemary now had the job of fixing supper every evening. That way, when her parents came home from work, they could all sit down and eat and have the rest of the evening free.

Rosemary walked back to the dining room. It had a bow window at one end that looked out over a city backyard. The spring evening was warm—like a summer night at home, Rosemary thought—and the window was open to catch any breeze. A huge ailanthus tree shaded the building, and Thompson sat close to the screen watching fascinated as the tree waved its fronds past him in a vagrant wind. How different it was here, Rosemary thought. Even the trees were different—at least here in the city they were —and the sounds were different too, in a subtle way. Instead of the occasional car you heard out on the street at home, there was a distant, steady roar of traffic here, and you had the sense of many more people around you as they returned from work and got supper and turned on the radio and called to each other.

And yet—it was funny—some things had remained pretty much the same. Tomorrow was Saturday, and as Rosemary used to meet Ruth, she would now meet Kelly in the afternoon after her Peabody classes, and they would see the same picture staring Judy Garland and Mickey Rooney that she might be seeing with Ruth—even from front-row seats!

And the newsreel showed the same horrors. On this particular Saturday there were pictures of the evacuation of the allied troops from Dunkirk.

"It's scary," said Rosemary. "Do you think we'll get in it?"

"I hope so," said Kelly. "Those Nazis have got to be stopped."

"Yes," said Rosemary. Nevertheless, moving pictures of a battle, seen in a theater, gave the matter a certain distance. She could not imagine war coming to the United States.

The next day was Sunday, and Rosemary went out to Kelly's again in the afternoon. Kelly played the piano, and they sang popular songs.

"Say, you know what? You have a pretty good voice," Kelly told her. "Did you ever think of taking lessons?"

"Vocal lessons? No," said Rosemary. But that wasn't strictly true. Ever since the operetta she *had* thought of it at times, and it hadn't seemed possible. Now she asked, "Do you think I should?"

"Sure. Why not? Why don't you apply at Peabody for the

fallsessionthn—maybeen some of the same ones."

Rosemary thought of the beautiful stone building on Mt. Vernon Place. Peabody made her think of famous musicians, of great talent—genius even—of kinds of music she knew nothing about. "They wouldn't take me there!" she said. "What do I know?"

"Oh, you poor fish!" said Kelly in exasperation. "That's where you *go* to know!"

"Well, I'll ask my parents," Rosemary said tentatively. But she was thrilled all the same. Whether she went to Peabody or did something else, the whole world seemed to be opening up for her.

After school closed for the summer, Rosemary and Kelly continued their friendship. They went to the library and picked out books together; they were constantly at the movies together; and they sang together, pretending they were in shows. One afternoon they went out to Fort McHenry and sat on the sea wall looking at the water and talking earnestly about their hopes and dreams.

But Rosemary often thought, too, about Lynnfield, about Ruth and her other friends there. Ruth wrote that she was seeing more of Franny and Ginger now. Their "thing" that summer was to spend their afternoons at the swimming pool at the Mountaintop Hotel just outside town. Ruth told Rosemary that when she came to visit later in the summer, they would take her with them and teach her how to play bridge, a game Ginger had initiated at poolside.

Because of Kelly, and occasional outings with Bernadette, Rosemary's homesickness had abated, but she still looked forward to her coming visit to Lynnfield in August with a passionate intensity.

And in due course August finally arrived. Early in the month her Aunt Jo came to visit them and announced that she was getting married in the fall and would be going to live in Washington, D.C. They would be practically neighbors, she said.

Lynnfield, however, was still Aunt Jo's home, and when, a week later, she went back there, Rosemary went with her.

Lynnfield . . . Lynnfield . . . the bus tires seemed to be saying that as they drove west, and Rosemary said the name with them over and over in her heart. By now Lynnfield had become for her a symbol of stability and of all that was permanent. Lots of things had happened to her, because she had gone away, but back there, she knew, her friends, the streets, the houses, everything would be exactly the same as she had left them, and always would remain so. Perhaps, she thought, when she got back there she would not go away again. Despite Kelly, despite Bernadette, despite the prospect of "voice" lessons, perhaps she would never go back to Baltimore.

18

When you leave a place for a while and then come back to it, having grown accustomed to other streets and houses, it has a strange look at first. You see it with unfamiliar eyes, and you see things that, perhaps, you never noticed when you were there every day. Lynnfield looked slightly out of focus to Rosemary as the bus drove into town, and it had an oddly different air, too, as later she and Aunt Jo drove through residential streets in the grandparents' car. She felt as if she were looking at it as it was reflected in a mirror, instead of directly, or as if, imperceptibly, it had moved half an inch up or down or to one side.

Funny . . . But it *was* the same, she was sure of that. Lynnfield and its inhabitants would never change. Perhaps *she* had changed, a little, because she had gone to a new place, seen new things, met new people. But the people in Lynnfield had just stayed where they were, so they could not have changed. . . .

Certainly her grandparents were the same, and as expected, her grandmother had prepared such an elaborate meal, with all of Rosemary's favorite dishes, that she couldn't just rush off and find Ruth immediately, although that was what she wanted to do. She sat at the table and told them all the news she thought they wanted to hear.

"Maybe we'll get to meet your new friend Kelly soon," her grandmother observed.

"Oh?" said Rosemary. "Are you coming down to see us?"

"No," said her grandmother.

"I'm being transferred to Hanover, P.A.," her grandfather put in. "I asked for it, as a matter of fact. We don't like being so far away from you and your mother, and Hanover will be a nice town for us to live in after I retire."

"Hanover's not far from Baltimore at all," her grandmother explained.

"For Pete's sake!" said Rosemary. "First Aunt Jo, now you. The whole family's moving away. There won't be anyone for me to stay with when I come up."

"I'm afraid not," said her grandfather, "not right in Lynnfield, anyway. You still have two other aunts, though."

"But they don't live in Lynnfield," Rosemary repeated mournfully.

"Well, don't worry about it, honey," her grandmother told her. "Ruth will still be here, and I'm sure she'll invite you for visits. Speaking of Ruth, she'll be coming any minute. I invited her up for dessert. I knew you two would be dying to see each other."

And just as she said that the doorbell rang.

"I'll get it!" Rosemary cried. She leaped from the table,

ran to the door, and threw it open. And there was Ruth, after all this time, dear Ruth, with her round face and her mischievous eyes, the same as ever.

"Hi!" They said it together, and they grinned at each other. Then they stood there; they couldn't think of an earthly thing to say.

Rosemary's grandmother saved the day by calling out, "Come on in, Ruth. You're just in time. I hope you like peach shortcake."

"Do I ever!"

Rosemary's grandfather pulled a chair out for Ruth, and she and Rosemary sat facing each other. They stared at each other, smiled, and continued to stare, and as they stared, Rosemary thought, She doesn't look the same, after all, not quite. What is it?

"Say," said Ruth. "I hope you can go swimming with us tomorrow."

"Of course she can," said Rosemary's grandmother. "I know you two want to spend as much time together as possible."

Eating the shortcake gave them something to do until they got used to each other again, and they quickly disposed of it. Rosemary's grandmother then told them to forget about the dishes this time, so they went outside into the early evening light and walked toward Ruth's house. It was still early enough for the sun to be above the mountaintops. Birds made muted twitterings in the trees overhead.

"I guess I told you my brother got married," Ruth said.

"Yes," said Rosemary.

177

"I have his room now; it's bigger than my old one."

"That's nice," said Rosemary. "You'll have more space for all your stuff."

They were coming within view of the Wakely house. The gate was open, and two cars were parked in the driveway. The girls stopped and peered in. Piles of lumber were lying around in several places. The front door was open, too, and the whole area—house and grounds—had an appearance of bustling activity.

"What's going on?" said Rosemary.

"Oh, I forgot to tell you. The house has been sold, and they're turning it into an apartment building—very ritzy, my mother says."

"But that's awful!" Rosemary protested.

"Yeah, I know," said Ruth. "It was more fun as a haunted house, wasn't it?"

"Well, it was certainly more interesting," said Rosemary.

They both sighed, then walked on a little way, and Rosemary said, "Er . . . have you seen Douglas?"

Ruth shook her head. "Not really. Once in a while I pass him on the street—not lately, though. I heard he was still going with that Kit Markey. She's kind of cute."

"Um," said Rosemary.

"Speaking of boys," Ruth said, "how are you going to manage in an all-girls school? I'd hate that."

"Well, *you* don't have to go to one," Rosemary pointed out. "Actually, it's not so bad."

"Everyone to her own taste," Ruth said airily. "Hey!" she added. "I've got a boyfriend—sort of."

"Oh? Who?"

"His name's Marty. He's new in town. He's a year older than I am, and he's a real dreamboat! His sister Wilma's nice too—she's my age, and she'll be in my class at high school next month."

"Oh?" said Rosemary.

"Yes. We've become real good friends."

"You never mentioned her in your letters."

"I figured you'd think I'd made her up—after you went on and on about that Kelly. Anyway," Ruth said, "you'll meet her and Marty tomorrow. They always go to the pool."

"Do they?" said Rosemary, her nose out of joint. "I can hardly wait."

The pool at the Mountaintop Hotel was of Olympic size, with bleachers on both sides for spectators at various water shows held at the hotel during the season. Between the bottom seats of the bleachers and the edge of the pool, metal tables and chairs, painted white, were tastefully arranged. Usually these tables were occupied by matrons of various ages who sat there absorbing the sun, drinking tall drinks, and playing cards.

Today, at one of those tables, however, sat Franny Stapleton and a sandy-haired girl named Wilma. Both girls were sitting sideways to the table, with their long legs stretched out toward the water, where they could take advantage of the sunlight. Franny got up when she saw Rosemary and hugged her. Wilma, upon being introduced, gazed up indifferently through hooded icy-blue eyes.

"They tell me you live in Baltimore now," she drawled. "I was there once. I didn't think much of it, though."

"Oh? Why not?"

"It's an awfully slow and pokey old place. You must know that if you live there," said Wilma. "I prefer New York myself."

"Oh . . . well . . . who doesn't?" said Rosemary, although she had never been to New York.

Wilma, who seemed chronically tired, reached lazily down into her beach bag and brought forth a pack of cards, a scorepad, and a pencil. She shuffled the cards expertly. "Are you kids ready to play?"

"Sure," said Ruth, "as soon as we teach the game to Rosemary."

"Oh, Lord!" said Wilma, looking pained. "You mean this child can't play bridge?" She might just as well have said, You mean this child can't spell *cat*?

"'Fraid not," said Rosemary without repentance. "Sorry." She had thought it would be jolly to learn to play bridge; now she no longer cared to. She would rather dive into the pool and swim—and get away from Wilma. The green water, rippled by a slight breeze and by the movements of the few swimmers who were in it, looked inviting on this hot day. Even the smell of chlorine brought back the flavor of summers past and added to her longing to be in the water.

Wilma sighed. "Well, let's teach her and get it over with," she said. She spread the cards out in a fan shape. "There are four of what we call suits," she explained, as if to a four-year-old. "This is a spade, this is a heart, this is—"

"I know that," Rosemary interrupted testily. She would feel so good, she thought, if she could just kick Wilma *hard*.

Ruth laughed. "Rosemary's not that dumb," she told Wilma. "She catches on to things fast." And she proceeded to explain to her the basic rules of bridge. "Come on," she said. "Let's play a hand. That's the best way to learn."

With Ruth as her partner, Rosemary soon felt fairly confident with the general play of the game, and even thought that under different circumstances she might have enjoyed it. She had a little trouble with the bidding, but it didn't take her long to realize that if she contrived to be the dummy, she got off the hook and her partner had to do the work. In fact, she was pleased to see, after a while, that she and Ruth were winning.

"Beginner's luck," Wilma said, gathering up the cards after she and Franny went down in a hand for the second time in a row. Her cold gaze drifted across the pool to the dressing-room door. "Oh, say, there's my brother," she said.

It was not only her brother. Two other boys, whom Rosemary knew only slightly, were with him. They all came over and stood around the table. There were perfunctory introductions and a rather overt appraisal of Rosemary's attributes, but apparently everybody had already paired off, after a fashion.

Marty stood behind Ruth and looked down at her cards. "Oh, what a good hand," he said. "I'd bid no trump if I were you, Ruth."

"Hey, cut that out!" Ruth hid her cards against her chest, but she didn't sound annoyed; she seemed pleased.

"We're trying to play a game here," Wilma said sternly. Her eyes had that hooded look, which seemed to be habitual, as she gazed up at the boy who stood next to her, but there was a flirtatiousness in the look now.

"We were getting along fine until you all turned up," said Franny. Suddenly she got up from her chair and pushed the third boy into the pool. The water arched up and splashed Wilma's legs.

"Yike!" she shrieked. "That's cold."

She had hardly had a chance to register the fact when Marty and her own boyfriend grabbed her, one by the shoulders, the other by the feet, swung her out, and tossed her into the water. They then turned toward Franny, who screamed, but got the same treatment, as did Ruth in turn. Meanwhile, Rosemary dived into the water herself. She had thought she'd never get a chance to cool off.

A lot of horseplay ensued, with much screaming and ducking. Rosemary waited in the deep end, treading water and feeling very much left out. Here she was, in her own hometown, with four people she had known to some degree all her life, two of them close friends, even, and she felt like a total stranger.

Marty swam out to her. "Hi, little girl," he said. "Why are you hiding here all by yourself?"

"I'm not hiding," said Rosemary.

"Yes, you are!" He splashed her gently and was about to duck her when Ruth suddenly appeared, grabbed him around the neck, and pulled him under. He came up coughing. "God, Ruth!" he said. "You almost drowned me! I'll get you for that."

Ruth yelled and swam away, fast, with Marty swimming after her.

Rosemary watched them for a bit, then lazily swam the width of the pool. Ruth hadn't wanted Marty to talk to her, she thought a little sadly.

The horseplay continued for a while; then Wilma, who had plainly made herself the leader of the group, climbed out of the water and dried herself off. "Come on, you guys," she called. "Cut it out. Let's play some more cards. We only have a couple more weeks to work on our suntans."

Gradually they all settled down and the game continued, but no one was really paying much attention to it now, Rosemary observed. The boys sat on the bleachers behind the table and made remarks about the girls; the girls, pretending they hadn't heard, made remarks back. Several times the wind blew the cards into the pool. The girls screamed and tried to hold them down, and the boys dived in after the lost cards, splashing everyone. Pretty soon the girls were playing with only part of a deck, and the game had to stop.

Through it all, Rosemary smiled and smiled. She didn't want anybody to think she disapproved or anything like that, because she didn't. It was just that Franny and Ruth, perhaps influenced by Wilma, seemed to have reached some plateau in life where she could not follow. She had always felt intimidated by boys, at least a little, and the ease they felt in this situation caused her to envy them and to feel like some country cousin, instead of a girl who now lived in a large city and who ought to have some poise.

At the time she left Lynnfield she and Ruth had been much the same in their lack of sophistication. In that regard, Rosemary hadn't changed, but Ruth had. Look at her leaning against Marty, Rosemary thought. Four months ago Ruth wouldn't have dreamed of doing that.

That night, as Rosemary lay in her grandparents' spare room underneath the picture of the stag at bay, she assessed herself and found herself wanting. She had the feeling that she would never be able to shriek and horse around the way the other girls did, because she really couldn't understand why boys liked it. Even if they did like it, she was sure she could never act like that—and especially not here. You had to feel very much at home to let yourself go, and the trouble was she didn't feel at home in Lynnfield anymore.

The next morning Rosemary walked down to see Mrs. Hauser. She found her former landlady sweeping the sidewalk in front of her house.

"Why, Rosemary as I live and breathe!"

"Yes, it's me, Mrs. Hauser."

"Well, how are you? How's your mother? Is she here with you?"

"She and Daddy will be here next week to take me back to Baltimore. I'm sure she'll stop by and see you."

Rosemary glanced over at the house across the street. She didn't have to say anything, because Mrs. Hauser understood. "I'm afraid Douglas is away this summer," she said. "He's been working in West Virginia. He'll be home in time for school, though. I'm sorry, Rosemary. I'm sure he'd have liked to have seen you."

No, he wouldn't, Rosemary thought. Well, it didn't matter. She would probably never see him again, anyway—or Mrs. Hauser, or Ruth, or Lynnfield itself.

She had a lost feeling in the pit of her stomach, but she smiled and said, "How's Malvina?"

"Oh, didn't you know? Arthur's mother died, so he and Malvina finally got married. She's been living over in the big house for over a month now."

"I'm so glad!" Rosemary said. "Not about Arthur's mother—but for Malvina. . . ."

Mrs. Hauser smiled. "I know what you mean, child."

"So . . ." said Rosemary. "I guess you have a lot of new roomers upstairs."

"No, as a matter of fact not," Mrs. Hauser told her. "We're fixing the place up now, so our daughter and her husband and baby can move in with us. We'd been talking about it for some time, and now we have the chance."

"That's nice," said Rosemary. But as she left Mrs. Hauser to her work, after promising to remind her mother to come down for a visit, she thought, everything has changed—*everything*—even the little unimportant things.

She passed Ruth's house again on her way back up the street. This time Ruth came out and said, "Oh, hi! Where've you been?" But without waiting for an answer, she added, "Swimming this afternoon?"

"Oh, sure, of course," said Rosemary. Might as well, she thought.

"OK," said Ruth. "We'll pick you up. Ginger and her brother are going today, too, and he's going to drive us."

"Good," said Rosemary. "It'll be nice to see Ginger."

But would it be? she wondered as she walked back to her grandparents' house for lunch. Ginger would no doubt be different too, and they would no longer have anything in common.

Rosemary supposed that if she were going to live here again, she would soon get back into the groove, but she wasn't going to live here. She wasn't a part of things now, and they all knew it. So what was the use?

Well, she could put up with it for a week or so. And then she would go back to Baltimore. There were all those Saturday afternoons and other projects with Kelly to look forward to, and school would soon start, too. This term she would no longer be new, but would start off the year with her class. Bernadette, for one, would be in it, and this time she would have a chance to meet more of the other girls— and maybe some of their brothers. . . .

Yes, she could stand being alone in a crowd for the rest of her visit, but this time, when she left Lynnfield, she would really be saying good-bye. She wasn't coming back. That was sad, of course, but life was like that, and for now, she just wanted to go home.

Carole Bolton says, "This book is loosely autobiographical (*very* loosely, I hasten to add). The town is pretty much as I remember, except for a few geographical changes, but the characters are mostly composites—Ruth and Mitch in particular.

"I suppose you might say Rosemary is a self-portrait, but that is only partially true. I was a much schleppier teenager than she is and even more movie-mad. I guess she is an idealized picture of myself as I would like to have been."

Ms. Bolton has written many books for young adults, including *Little Girl Lost* and *The Search of Mary Katherine Mulloy*, and has been a children's book editor. She lives in Montville, Maine.